D1575294

THE
PORTER ROCKWELL
CHRONICLES
VOL. 3

OTHER BOOKS BY THE AUTHOR:
Porter Rockwell: A Biography (1986)
Rockwell: U.S. Marshal, A Novel (1987)
The Porter Rockwell Chronicles, Vol. 1 (1999)
The Porter Rockwell Chronicles, Vol. 2 (2000)

Richard Lloyd Dewey

THE
PORTER ROCKWELL
CHRONICLES

Vol. 3

STRATFORD
B O O K S

The Porter Rockwell Chronicles
Vol. 3

Book Cover Painting: Al Rounds

Book Cover Design: Vance Hawkins

ISBN: 0-9616024-8-1
The Porter Rockwell Chronicles, Vol. 3

Stratford Books, L.C.
Eastern States Office
4308 37th Road North
Arlington, Virginia 22207

Stratford Books, L.C.
Western States Office
P.O. Box 1371
Provo, UT 84603-1371

First Printing: October, 2001

This book is printed on acid-free paper.

Printed in the United States of America

*To the Hole in the Wall Gang of 1973-1974, who first inspired
me with mid-summer night stories about Porter Rockwell,
which launched me on my path of research:*
Clark Price
Jim Raines
Chuck Wilcher
Bill Cochard
Dave Hatton
Chuck Larson
Don Lamb
Daniel Lewis
Hamik Gregory
John Hoopes
Dan Morris
Sam Webb

*The downstairs boys: Dan Mangum, Ed Spann, Lamont
Worden, Danny Nelson, etc.*

*Our fearless leader, Boyd Erickson, and any others my
memory fails to recall a quarter century later.*

FOREWORD

Volume 3 is a continuation of Porter Rockwell's life story, wrapping up the Nauvoo period and, as with the first two volumes, is told with as much historical accuracy as possible for historical fiction. It is also designed to serve as an early history of the events surrounding the Mormon movement.

Because of Rockwell's relationship with early leaders, he was eye-witness to most historically significant scenes.

Volumes 3 and 4 of the *Chronicles* possess a certain amount of material similar to the author's previous work published in 1987, a relatively small novel entitled, "Rockwell: U.S. Marshal, A Novel." However, these *Chronicles* explore his relationships with greater dilineation and present considerably more dramatic scenes and historical information.

PART I

Liberty

CHAPTER 1

Riding until dawn, Porter fell asleep in thick woods. Shimmering green leaves and a warm howling wind greeted him as he awakened in bright daylight. He had bid farewell to his mother, brothers and sisters, then Ugly had followed him a mile out of town, until Porter had sent him back.

"I'll see you sometime, Ugly," he said. "You take care of my mama. Now get back to the house."

The dog sadly, obediently turned and ambled away, and stopped to study Porter one last time as his master disappeared on his horse around a bend in the road.

Across Midwestern meadows Porter walked beside his horse, not wishing to tire it. It was a true, old friend he always treated with respect. Another sunset found him stewing over his wife and children — and the future. He camped down for the night and stared into his fire. He talked to his horse and admired its handsome but weathered features. They had been through a lot together.

The journey took him eastward, across the entire state of Illinois, through the breadth of Indiana, and into Ohio. There, he stopped at several villages to find employment.

No one needed help and the general economy was not conducive to hiring, people said, yet he kept trying.

At Hamden, Ohio he attempted to visit his sisters Caroline and Emily again, but they were out of town for several weeks. His attempts at procuring employment there also proved fruitless. He decided to move on, feeling distraught that his last visit with Caroline several years earlier may have been his last. Over the campfire on the road East that night it hurt him how transient life was, and how the enduring relationships of childhood and adolescence could so change. At one time everything seemed locked into a secure world. He realized now how not only his world of siblings but his own children's world had at such an early age turned upsidedown. Tears glistened on his cheeks.

He arrived at the Atlantic, and was met by the intoxicating scent of Atlantic sea breezes. He walked with his horse on the sand and gazed at the cloud-covered stormy waters. He felt an impending excitement as he neared the crashing waves. At the edge of the ocean he dismounted and stared at the Eastern horizon. It was a heavily overcast late afternoon on which he sauntered southward with his horse, unable to take his eyes off the ocean waves. The sound of their fury seemed to blend with the emotions pounding in his soul.

Outside Philadelphia he applied at several farms. Two farmers were willing to hire him only for food.

He set out on foot into the city, sleeping alongside the road at night and applying at every farm he passed.

Two days later he arrived in Philadelphia and went directly to Samuel Armstrong's home. There, years earlier, he and Joseph had visited during the Washington D.C. trip. He left his horse in their fenced back yard to eat all it wanted. As one of the few families of faith in the city, Armstrong literally welcomed Porter with open arms. His wife kissed him with a warm greeting on the cheek. To his surprise, before him in their small but tidy home, were four children — approximating the ages of his own. He almost gasped when he noticed how much they also resembled them.

But just before entering, he was introduced to a neighbor who had recently read anti-Mormon tracts and threatened Armstrong. With Porter there, the neighbor suddenly ceased his taunts. With his intense demeanor and tragic aura developed in recent years, Porter's imposing, muscular, stocky structure and serious, solid face came across to most as terribly intimidating. Indeed, he seemed to many a walking weapon.

The next morning Porter enjoyed crisp, sugar-cured, smoked bacon and eggs, prepared by Sister Armstrong from their small farm, and he left before sunrise to search for work.

In the mercantile district he asked at one factory after another. No one was hiring—the economy was barely hanging on. He spent the night in a stranger's barn.

In his hosts' home the next day he was welcomed again, but the delicious meal of sausage gravy and eggs over fresh biscuits was difficult to eat. He kept looking at Armstrong' kids. Samuel invited him to assist in working the farm for food, as he had little cash. Porter thanked him but declined, wanting to help for free every other day, when he was not looking for employment. As he watched the children play after supper, he felt pained.

Armstrong sensed his discomfort and asked if he could help. Porter shook his head and tried for a smile.

That night Armstrong awoke to find Porter in the front room in tears, holding the youngest child and hugging her. The next day Porter then helped his host on the farm lifting heavy fence posts into holes he had dug.

Again it saddened him to see the children watching him at supper.

The next two days he stayed away, searching for work and sleeping in others' barns with the owners' permission. On the third day he arrived in the commercial district early. At the first place he entered at dawn, the proprietor shook his head. And at the 20th place he passed at sundown, he was met with the same response.

Dejected, he returned to the Armstrong's and stared into the fireplace until he fell asleep on the floor. The next day he chopped Armstrong's wood, unable to face another day of rejection. But the following day, seeing Armstrong's children was again too painful, so he decided to look for employment.

At dawn he trudged up the road. He did not realize how his countenance disconcerted not only most strangers but also prospective employers. They were mostly polite to him, but would often stare as he'd walk away, and sometimes shake their heads. His dour expression, born by the frustration of finding no employment and the agony of missing his family and friends, actually frightened them.

One widow answered her farmhouse door, took one look at his face, and screamed.

Porter blinked, could think of nothing to say, blinked again, turned and walked off.

The woman, embarrassed, apologized, but Porter just kept walking.

CHAPTER 2

"**W**rite a letter for me, would you please?" said Porter, entering Armstrong's home that night.

"To whom?"

"My wife and family."

Armstrong did. Afterwards, Porter asked him to write Joseph a letter telling him he was safe in Philadelphia. He then left to wander the streets and think, leaving Armstrong to compose the letter.

Armstrong helped put the children to bed, sat at his table, and wrote by candlelight:

"Dear Brother Joseph Smith, I am requested by our friend Orrin Porter Rockwell to drop a few lines informing you that he is in this place. His health is good, but his spirits are depressed, caused by his being unable to obtain employment of any kind. He has applied in different parts of the city and country, but all without success, as farmers can get persons to work from sunrise till dark for merely what they eat.

"He is most anxious to hear from you, and wishes you to see his mother and write all the particulars, how matters and things are and what the prospects are. I pity him from the bottom of my heart. His lot in life seems marked with sorrow, bitterness, and care. He is a noble, generous friend. But you know his worth: Any comments from me would be superfluous. He will wait in this place till he hears from you. Please write immediately, as it will be a source of great comfort to him to hear.

"If Joseph is not at home, Brother Whitney will be kind enough to write. Porter says every other one [Mormon] he has come across here has been afraid of their shadows, but he watches them well. He comes to see me every other day, and I keep him close!

"Answer this as soon as received. Yours truly, S. Armstrong for Orrin Porter." (Author's note: This was the actual text of Armstrong's letter.)

After finishing voluntary chores for Armstrong the next few weeks while simultaneously searching for work, one day Porter went to several larger farms across town. The answers were the same. He finally retreated into his thoughts: He went directly to the ocean an hour before sunset and sat on a rock. There, he found a strange comfort in the concert of the crashing waves: They seemed to understand his turmoil.

He studied a man playing with his daughter, a year or two from Emily's age and with the same color hair. The man, merely a hundred feet away, tossed her into the air several times, both laughing. Porter walked on, hearing the plaintive cry of sea gulls, unable to watch the scene further.

As he strolled along the beach the waves rose higher. How easy, he thought, it would be to just walk into the sea — and keep going. His soul felt nothing to live for without his family, especially Emily. Despite Luana's declarations to the contrary, she might keep his children from him forever, he realized, and Emily would grow up a stranger. But he had to stay alive for Emily's sake. For all the kids' sakes.

When the sun set into a gray, cold horizon, he pulled his blankets from a bag, curled into them warmly, and slept by the shore, the rocking rhythm of the sea lulling him to sleep. Upon awakening at dawn he washed his face in the salty water, and turned inland, impressed with a feeling he'd never again see the Atlantic.

CHAPTER 3

At the Armstrong cabin he entered before sunset. Samuel was still awake.

"You got a letter," said Samuel.

Porter strode to a heavy chair, not taking his eyes from him.

"Would you like me to read it?" said Armstrong.

"Who's it from?"

"Joseph."

Porter's eyes brightened.

Armstrong smiled and opened it, then began reading:

"Dear Brother Porter,

"You may wish to know that conditions have not changed, and safety is still at the forefront of my concerns. Your children seem happy, yet I see that Emily, especially, misses you. Not many months hence and your reunion with her should be sweet indeed. Luana seems pleasant and comfortable.

"Your mother and siblings are well. The city is prospering even more than before.

"When it is safe for you to return, I shall obtain for you, if you so desire, employment as a taxi driver for Amos Davis' one-horse taxi. You may also find room and board at his hotel. This will allow you to not have to farm, but rather labor at something you no doubt would enjoy.

"Perhaps our next step could be to save our funds and secure for you your own ferry operation!

"Please be of good cheer and persevere. This life's trials prepare us for greater mansions elsewhere, as you indicated at the river bank. Remember, we all love you greatly.

"Your friend always,

"Joseph."

Porter's face lit up. He stood.

"That's it," said Porter. "That is the key."

"What key? To what?"

"The mystery."

"What're you talking about?" said Armstrong.

"I've spent a lot of time at the ocean, and I've stared at the stars and figured a key to my future has to be somewhere. That letter is the key."

"What does it say to you?"

"That it's time to go back." Porter nodded. "Yes, sir. That's what it says."

"Porter, I don't believe it says that exactly. In fact, if I read correctly, it says he'll contact you when it is safe to return."

"Can't you see? It's clear . . ."

"Perhaps your pain is persuading you," said Armstrong.

"The letter is."

"But the law is still after you, isn't it?"

Porter began packing his gear. His countenance revealed a hope for the first time since Armstrong had seen him.

"Yep, it's very clear," said Porter.

"Aren't you concerned for the law?"

"Joseph will get the laws changed so the city charter will protect us again."

"What do you mean?"

"I mean with the charter in place again we can't be extradited to Missouri."

"Couldn't it be weeks before Joseph's lawyers fix that system?" said Armstrong. "You told me yourself when you first got here that the Illinois officials are now cooperating with Missouri. So aren't you afraid Missouri deputies will come for you?"

Porter got angry. "Trouble is, they'll never catch me. And if they did, maybe I'd enjoy taking on a few." In addition to his family needing him, the idea of running Davis' taxi in Nauvoo excited him: It was a long-overdue emotional renaissance from the tedium of farm work to which he'd felt enslaved for half a decade. And, compared to here, at least it was work. More than that — he saw it as enjoyable employment, similar in some respects to the river barge. He enjoyed dealing with passengers and hosting strangers, and the thought crossed his mind he would not mind owning an inn someday like Davis's. As for the taxi, he also saw it as an opportunity to keep an eye on the city for Joseph — to see which strangers were coming and going. It would therefore enhance his ability to protect Joseph. He could not wait to return and feel useful again.

There was a long pause.

"We'll miss you, Porter," said Armstrong, seeing Porter could not be dissuaded.

Armstrong felt saddened to see him leave — he'd developed a bond with him. He loaded Porter down with jerky and bread to send him on his way.

Porter stood erect and breathed easier.

"You know, Brother Armstrong, for all my hard times, I see I'm finally being blessed. My family's still in Nauvoo. Luana will have me back. I see a lifetime of things going good for me and our people. After all we've seen and gone through. Spring has finally broken."

Armstrong sat back, placed his hands behind his head and stretched. He was hopeful for his new friend, yet fearful:

"In all honesty I hoped you'd be able to stay. I'm close to losing my farm. My horse is old, and I figured between the two of us we could plow."

Porter noticed tears flowing from Armstrong's wife. She turned so Porter could not see them. He gazed out the back window at his horse. After a few moments he arose. "Take him."

"What?" said Armstrong.

"You heard me. I don't need my horse as much as you. 'Looks like I won't be farming with him anyway once I get back home."

Armstrong nodded, in shock.

"So it's yours," said Porter with a smile.

It nearly broke his heart to part with it, but he had to. He looked upon this family as his own — yet with physical rather than emotional challenges — and where his father had once helped him with the money for the barge, it was his turn to pass along blessings to a similar family. He patted his horse on the nozzle one last time. Its eyes looked as sad as he himself felt. The animal sensed it was parting from its finest, old friend forever. Porter realized it had been his favorite horse he could remember, of the four he and his family had owned since he was a child. This one he'd had for himself since the barge years, and it even reminded him of those beautiful days on the river, the last token in fact of that era. It had been born from his parents' old farm horse they had brought west from New York, and he had raised it since a colt. As he walked away, he turned back to stare at it, and finally left for good, his heart pounding.

Armstrong, his wife and four children stared appreciatively at Porter and waved tearfully as their rugged friend, a hundred yards down the dusty dawn road, turned his head one last time and waved back. They had become quite attached to the old warrior. It was the last time he knew he would ever see the Armstrong family, or his horse, and they stood there seemingly frozen in time. It was a poignant scene he'd never forget.

A bittersweet smile suddenly enveloped him for the first moment in many months. He would take passage on the Eerie Canal. At Lake Eerie he would transfer to an overland route, walking crude paths until he'd make his way south to the Ohio River and there board a steamboat with his last coins that would take him to the Mississippi River.

That would be his course the next few weeks, but for the moment he could only enjoy the feeling of freedom from despair, and actually feel pure hope.

He glanced up at the orange color from the setting sun reflecting off gray clouds, on to the road ahead. He felt a gentle breeze on his face. His nostrils took in a whiff of fresh air from the nearby tree-lined Pennsylvania meadow. Life was, after all, pretty darn fair.

Spring had indeed broken.

CHAPTER 4

$\mathbf{A}$s the steamboat moved its way lazily up the Mississippi, it was an unseasonably warm late winter evening of 1843. Porter stared at the currents, lost in his thoughts over ten year old daughter Emily.

As he felt the river's gentle breeze, he flirted with thoughts of his wife taking him back. The primary problem she had with him of late seemed to have evolved into his "outlaw image," disseminated through articles in area newspapers and territorial wanted posters.

He was confident that news about him had died down while he had spent the previous few months in Philadelphia; however, he was certain that he was still wanted for the attempted assassination of former Governor Lilburn Boggs, and knew he must keep a low profile.

Knowing he was innocent of the Boggs shooting was especially frustrating, because he had just taken material steps to patching up marital problems with his wife before he had become the target of so much bad press.

Anxious to return and clear his name among family and friends, he nevertheless wondered for a fleeting moment if this were not a premature jump from the East Coast. But he had spent most of his last money on steamboat fare to return to Nauvoo, so there was now no turning back.

Looking over the railing, he felt drowsy and peaceful, and decided to retire to his small cabin below deck.

As he lay on the bunk, he vaguely made out the sound of footsteps outside the door. He grabbed his pistol and cocked it. He quickly donned his boots. He would not normally be so cautious, but suspected that the closer he came to St. Louis — the destination of his boat journey until he could transfer to Nauvoo — the more likely would be his chances of being recognized by a bounty-hunter. He knew the reward money on his hide was higher now, but did not realize it had actually doubled to $3,000.

He finished with his boots and eased to the door. He thought he felt the presence of someone just outside. He slowly turned the knob, then swung it open.

No one.

He walked slowly up to the deck. He could see the moonlight glittering across the water. He felt the cooling air of the peaceful evening. Suddenly he heard someone behind him. He whirled around and caught glimpse of a shadowed figure swinging his fist towards him. But before he could react, he felt a crashing thud against his jaw. He reeled back and saw his assailant grasp his own right hand — his knuckles broken from their attack on Porter's jaw. As is generally the case, when a man's fist connects with another's jaw, the fist loses, despite what dime novels of his day reported when fictionalizing fist fights.

Porter recovered from the jolt and dove towards his assailant. He grabbed the man's other hand and smashed it against the gunwale. The man screamed and began running. Porter ran forward and tackled him. He turned the man over and could see his face clearly in the moonlight. It was a stranger — tall and bearded — with the clothes of a gentleman.

"What do you want of me?" said Porter.

"Nothing," the man growled.

Porter searched the stranger's vest and pulled out folded papers. He held them under the moonlight and, though he could not read, recognized a crude portrait of himself on one — a wanted poster.

"Where'd you get this?" said Porter.

"Where do you think?"

"I wouldn't be askin' if I knew."

"Most any marshal's office will have 'em," said the man, nursing his two wounded hands as well as possible and flinching under the pain. "If you're interested, I'm sure they'll let you take a couple," he added dryly.

"Where were you planning to take me?"

"You don't need to ask so many questions."

"You a bounty hunter?" said Porter.

"Figure it out for yourself."

Porter gazed into the man's eyes. "Can you swim?"

"Why?"

The bounty hunter found himself being tossed over the gunwale and splashing into the water.

"Ain't more than fifty yards to shore," shouted Porter. "But the water's a little brisk, so I reckon you best get to pumpin'.

The man swore and began swimming.

Porter smiled as he saw the fellow stagger to shore a few minutes later. He wondered if the bounty hunter would continue the chase, alert someone else, or just give up all together.

Porter returned to his cabin and tossed on his bunk for an hour, worrying though exhausted. He figured to be just hours from Nauvoo, first having to stop at St. Louis.

He also knew he had more than a fair chance at winning back Luana and his family. He had the momentum of positive experiences with her, ever since they had returned to Nauvoo together from her parents. If he could only spend additional time with her in these next, crucial days and weeks, he figured he could win her heart again. He was certain of that.

The next day, March 4, 1843, he stepped off the riverboat at St Louis. The late winter winds, still unseasonably warm, began to howl. He needed to make only the last leg of the journey — but first had to go unrecognized at the dock. Walking to the ticket hut, he showed his ticket that would enable him to transfer to the steamboat heading for Nauvoo.

With his hat pulled low he waited at dockside. Within minutes the boat would arrive and take him across the wide Mississippi and up-river. The 165 mile journey would take the better part of a day. He glanced about for any suspicious faces. Two dozen people moved about their business and no one seemed concerned.

He could finally see the steamer that would take him to Nauvoo. He watched it coming closer. He would be boarding first. He felt an anxiousness overtake him. In his mind he could see his children. He picked up each one. They were everything to him and he could not wait to kiss them . . . especially Emily. Then suddenly a flash of steel cut into the small of his back.

He gasped.

Elias Parker had not possessed sufficient skills to become a county sheriff, due in part to his lack of education, and resultant inability to fill out paperwork, but he did exude the confidence of a bonified bounty hunter of outlaws. Parker was Porter Rockwell's height, but considerably trimmer. He wore a handlebar moustache and a stunning, white leather hat. He marched Porter through the streets of St Louis amidst crowds of curious on-lookers, including several other bounty hunters. However, none but Parker, and the river boat bounty hunter, had been able to match the face of this prisoner to the printed wanted poster plastering the city. And that suited Parker just fine. He did not want Porter to have attracted competition. He was proud of the fact he was bringing the notorious Mormon outlaw in, but equally pleased that such a healthy reward had been posted and would soon be his.

As they walked around a corner, Porter noticed a pile of boards ahead. He grabbed one sticking out beside him and, in one motion, whirled it up and behind. It smashed Parker's gun away. Porter jumped on his captor and fisted him in the stomach, then jumped to the board and grabbed it.

Elias Parker awakened an hour later, just after dark. His whole body was sore, and he rubbed his stomach. He stood curiously and looked around.

Porter had returned to the dock and was waiting for another barge. The ticket master was honoring his unused ticket. His mind drifted to the ultimate freedom. He felt it would not be much longer till he arrived there. He felt a gentle breeze on his face, and reflected on what it would be like to see Joseph again, and to talk with Luana and especially to hug the kids. He craved the sight of the beautiful, tree-lined streets of his friends' homes in Nauvoo, and good, home-cooked meals again. His spirits were soaring. Across the river and up a day at Nauvoo, he thought he could envision children on the river bank recognizing and greeting him, surprised to see his early return. He would see his own children's faces minutes later. Then Luana's. She seemed to speak with a different voice, and spoke words uncharacteristic of her. The vision suddenly disappeared and re-appeared as a stranger, with different colored hair. She walked, speaking, as if in a trance towards him, and stopped. She saw someone behind Porter and she walked to that man and hugged him. Porter awakened from his reverie in a cold sweat. He feared what Luana was doing.

Suddenly he heard that stranger's voice, and turned. Standing before him in the cold, stark world of reality, was a deputy sheriff sporting a sparkling tin badge. Standing beside the deputy was Elias Parker once again. Porter was angry with himself for not tying up Parker until the steamer had departed.

"You sure that's him?" said the deputy, peering at Porter in the torchlight on the dock.

"Yeah, I am," said Parker. "Look at this poster for yourself."

The deputy then held up a double-barreled shotgun and aimed it straight at Porter's chest. "Tie his wrists behind his back. Tie 'em tight."

CHAPTER 5

Porter was actually surprised to find a mob had gathered. He didn't appreciate a fraction of his notoriety. The rowdier element of the townspeople had received word of his arrival and was shouting in a frenzy.

James Fox, Deputy Sheriff of St. Louis, had stayed with him from the moment of his arrest in St. Louis to his present transfer to Independence, Missouri; yet, even the deputy was more than a little surprised at the outlaw's reception. For a moment Fox feared for his own life as the stagecoach pulled into the midst of the screaming throng.

Porter was now 29 and tanned, with a chest and arms like a grizzly bear's.

Five dozen men screamed for his blood and a hangman's noose was passed over their heads. Deputy Fox stepped out of the stage with his revolver cocked, intending to protect his prisoner if it killed him. Porter saw him trembling. Porter mumbled, "'Bet *your* fan club ain't this big."

Fox fired a shot in the air, and blew the glass off a lamppost. Several men stepped back, not so much fearing him, Porter thought to himself, but afraid he was a horrible shot.

To Porter's relief, the town sheriff stepped out of his office and came forward. He yelled at the mob to get out of the way and marched up to the stagecoach door.

"Get out," he said to Porter.

"Only if you're a better shot than him," said Porter.

Reynolds smiled and grabbed Porter as he came out the stagecoach door. He then handcuffed Porter and led him into the street.

With Porter beside him Sheriff Reynolds made his way through the screaming mob to the jail. He clanged the door shut behind his prisoner.

Inside the jailhouse, Porter entered a stone room with a wooden floor and urine-drenched hay. The mob was now chanting something about hanging him.

Flies buzzed loudly. He pushed the hay aside and sat on moist wood. The room was chilled. Soon he began shivering. In near-darkness he stared at the faint rays of moonlight seeping under the door cracks.

He wondered if he ever again would see Luana and the kids.

The mob now shouted at their sheriff but, seeing it amounted to no avail, finally dispersed.

Three days passed and the door shot open. Since he had been fed only small amounts of bread and water, he was weak. Sheriff Reynolds escorted him outside into the blinding light.

The mob had returned. They shouted and spat at him as he walked to the courthouse two blocks away.

Inside, his court convened. The magistrate glared at him, listening to Deputy Sheriff Fox.

"Get Governor Boggs here," said Fox.

"What's your purpose?" said the judge.

"Governor Boggs swears Porter shot him," said Fox.

"The former governor is still recovering from gunshot wounds . . . in the back of his head," added the judge with a sniff. "He obviously never saw the assailant."

"Well, Porter 'fessed up to me himself that he shot him," said Fox.

A loud mumble rolled through the courtroom.

"What proof 'you got?" said the judge.

Fox said nothing.

Finally, Porter broke the silence. "I never shot Boggs, your honor."

"And what's your proof?"

Porter knew they were aware of his shooting abilities — he had won matches from Missouri to New York. But all he could do was stare at the judge, thinking of a credible answer.

Deputy Fox darted his eyes across the courtroom, sensing by half the courtroom a certain halted admiration for the outlaw and by others pure contempt. All waited for the reply.

"I will repeat my question," said the judge. "What is your proof you did not shoot Governor Boggs?"

"Well, your honor," said Porter, "My best buddy Joseph Smith asked me the same thing. All I could tell him is this, 'You wonder if *I* shot him? He's still alive, ain't he?'"

Half the courtroom burst into laughter. The other half still seethed at his very presence. The judge fought to hold back a smile. The prisoner's innate honesty and impeccable reputation for frankness in his earlier years in Independence had an impact on both the judge and half the people. But political forces were at work to keep him longer than he had ever anticipated . . .

CHAPTER 6

$\mathbf{A}$s Porter was escorted back to the county jail, the jailer confided, "They've found no crime against you."

"So why am I here?"

"Safekeeping."

"Can you take off the irons?"

"That's up to Sheriff Reynolds."

The jailer was a slight, heavily-mustached, and stoop-shouldered city servant who always carried out his work with clinical precision. His boss, Sheriff Reynolds, was an impassioned entity who sought not only law and order but eventual civic aspirations. Reynolds had hoped to be appointed to a high-standing, life-long, secure position within the Missouri state government, free from the vacillating whims of voters who could dash him out of office from damaging rumors or bad press. At 37, he was a large, looming figure who always seemed to be looking down at you, even if he were sitting. He had a large, square head and fat lips. Privately, Reynolds found as the years went on that he enjoyed living alone, and though he kept his distance from the townspeople, he was often asked to dinner, not for his position particularly, but because he was simply worth his salt.

Inside the cell Porter waited another day before food was finally brought. Nevertheless, even with the arrival of the food, the iron hobbles remained clamped to his feet and hands.

Another five days passed before he saw the jailer's face. Finally, twelve days later, the sheriff himself arrived.

"I'm half frozen every night," said Porter. "Can you build me a fire?"

"Too busy," said the sheriff.

"What about the handcuffs?"

"You'll survive."

"Why am I being kept here?"

"Waiting for the judge's decision."

"And how long will that be?"

"'Long as it takes."

"Then can you loose my hands a little till he decides?" "What's the matter — you itch in places you wished you didn't?" Reynolds chuckled and tromped away from Porter.

"What does the judge have to decide?" said Porter.

"Nothing. It's up to the prosecuting attorney now to find something. Are you satisfied? You think it's every day we hold a prize pig this big?" Reynolds slammed the door behind him.

Porter was not only itching, his stomach was cramping. Furthermore, he was aching from his ever-present obsession.

An autumn and a winter had passed since he'd hugged Luana and the four children. Philadelphia had been the loneliest spot on earth, he reflected. Till now. His mind remained riveted to Luana, his four children, his friends, and even his dog, Ugly.

He was taken upstairs each day, but at night would be confined to the basement dungeon.

During the last week of April he would alternately bake from the mid-day heat and freeze from the evening cold.

What added to his discomfort were his waste problems; his hands were still cuffed behind his back.

Nevertheless, his arms had ceased to cramp. His stocky frame had taken on a skeletal look. Inside, his worries for his family were contorting his mind. He even wondered if Luana had found another man.

On the morning of his 30th birthday, June 28th, 1843, he beheld a stranger entering his cell. He was tall and gaunt, about his own age. He stood directly over Porter.

"I've never been in jail before," sniffed the stranger.

Porter grunted.

"Don't reckon I've ever been locked up with a criminal before either," added the stranger.

"Neither have I," said Porter.

"My name's Watson."

"What're you in for?" said Porter.

"Counterfeiting."

He was pale in hair, face, arms, and even his eyes. He even spoke in a pale voice with tones cultivated by literate parents.

That night neither man slept. The next morning Watson broke the long silence. "Where would I find the outhouse around here?"

"You're layin' in it."

Watson moved across the room and gazed at Porter. "Have you considered escaping from this hole?"

"Naw, they'll let me out sooner or later."

"Later, from what I understand," said Watson.

"What do you understand?"

"If you escape with me, I'll tell you."

"No chance," said Porter. "I'm gettin' out soon."

"That's what you think."

CHAPTER 7

The next afternoon, Sheriff Reynolds entered and removed Porter's cuffs, then led Watson away.

Porter heard a clang on the window bar. He glanced outside and spotted a small, black girl on the street below, holding a covered basket. She had thrown the rock to get his attention. She tossed him a whip stock with a long piece of twine attached to it.

With this "fishing pole" Porter drew up the mysterious basket. When he uncovered it, he discovered a dozen pieces of freshly fried chicken. He nearly passed out from the aroma. He picked up a warm leg and rotated it in his hand, observing its perfect, flaky, crispness. He could feel the warm meat through the delectably fried, cornbread skin. He placed it almost worshipfully back into the basket.

He glanced suspiciously down at the girl outside. "Where'd you get this?"

"Ain't your business, mister."

"Yeah it is — I'm eatin' it."

"Then do it at your own risk," she said, strutting away.

"Wait a minute," said Porter.

"I can't tell you," she snapped, still walking. "So take it or leave it."

"But who sent it?"

"I said all you need to hear," she finally offered, disappearing.

"Humble child," mumbled Porter to himself.

Watson was absent, still in court, as Porter perused the chicken. The counterfeiter presently returned.

"I don't know when I'm being released from here," said Watson. "That judge is insane. What's that smell?"

Porter produced the basket from behind his back.

Watson's eyes bulged.

Porter threw him a piece of chicken.

Watson tore into it, chewed it as if he had not eaten in years, and swallowed. Then noticed Porter staring at him. "Well?" said Watson.

"Well, what?"

"What are you staring at?"

"Nothin'," said Porter.

"What do you mean 'nothin'? You're staring at me."

"Don't talk, just eat." Porter threw him another piece.

Watson chewed, glanced up, and noticed Porter still staring at him. "Why are you still looking at me!"

"Just seein' if you're all right."

"How am I doing?"

"Just fine."

Watson glared. "Why the devil do you care!"

"I want to see if this here chicken's poisoned. So far you seem all right."

Watson sighed and glanced down. "You're a real gentleman. 'You know that?"

"Yep," agreed Porter. "Who else would share you half his southern fried, fresh, un-poisoned chicken?" And at that he tore off another piece and threw it at Watson.

Watson caught it, smiled, and dug in. Porter studied him another minute before Watson caught him again staring. Porter winked and began eating.

The next day, Porter fastened a hard corn-dodger to the "fishing pole" twine and lowered it to the street below.

Strolling Missourians stopped and stared.

"What are you doing?" said Watson to Porter.

"Come over here."

Watson moved across the cell and looked out the window. Below, a crowd of eight men and four women were gathering and staring up at them, baffled. Porter bobbled the corn dodger in front of their faces and laughed. The pedestrians moved on, but soon another group clustered and stared.

Watson returned to his corner of the cell. "You have a strange sense of humor, my friend."

Porter was amused by their faces. "I reckon so," he said, still staring at them, then he began chuckling. "You're boring as sin, so I gotta get entertained some way or other."

A lightning storm unleashed with a ferocity Porter had never seen. He was awakened by the first flash, then noticed, from several more flashes, Watson staring at the ceiling. Moments later, thunderous crashes shook the air. After a long silence, Watson spoke. "Could this be a sign?"

"I know what you're thinkin'," said Porter. "Just get the thought out of your head."

"So you expect to stay in this trap?"

"You ain't gettin' me holed up for life," said Porter, "so don't even think it another minute."

"If you knew what I know about you — and what they're planning for your friend, Smith — you'd be surprised."

"What're you talkin' about?"

"They came to see Sheriff Reynolds the other day," said Watson.

"Who?"

"Conspirators against your friend."

"When I first came here I overheard them downstairs. They want to do away with him."

"I've heard that before," said Porter. "Everybody's tried — everybody's failed."

"I'm just telling you what I heard. And I could tell you more."

Porter figured Watson was inventing the story to incentivise his participation in the jail break.

"I ain't going. I'll be out of jail soon enough if I don't foul up. So no escapes, understand?"

"My friend, you are dreaming. They plan to keep you here forever, and use you for bait. 'Seems to me you should find out who's planning all this, and save your friend. I could give you a few leads."

Porter dismissed the statement and closed his eyes. The rain came harder.

"A couple of Joseph's closest associates — his own people — are plotting it. You break jail with me, and I'll tell you everything I know."

Porter gave him a skeptical look.

Watson re-emphasized his point. "Good behavior won't get you out — I will."

Porter thought another minute. This could be his one chance to return to Luana and the children weeks earlier than otherwise — before she takes up with a new man. Another flash of lightning hit even closer, and the thunder crashed immediately afterwards.

That evening Porter and Watson waited for the jailer to return for dishes.

"You shouldn't have ate so much," said Porter.

"I've been starving — what do you expect?"

"To eat just enough."

"I'll eat what I please," said Watson.

They finally heard the jailer clumping up the stairs. As the door opened, the two prisoners sprang to the door, grabbed the jailer and shoved him inside. They locked the door and ran down the stairs.

The jailer's wife saw them downstairs and screamed.

The two men ran outside. As they passed the garden, Porter tossed the key into it. He saw 20 yards ahead a board fence 12 feet high. They ran towards it and began climbing.

Porter scrambled to the top first, glanced below, and saw Watson still struggling half way up.

"Go ahead, I'll catch you," said Watson.

"I told you — you shouldn't have ate so much," said Porter.

"Stop nagging me, and don't worry, I'll catch you!"

Porter dropped to the other side and took off running. After a few seconds he turned and looked back. Watson's face was bobbling above the fence, grunting to get over.

Across town, gathering outside a tavern now, were a dozen Missourians who had been alerted by the jailer's wife. Porter spotted them and glanced back at the fence. Watson was finally calling for his help. Porter glanced at the mob again. It was gathering in size and beginning to run towards them. He had to make a choice: If he made a dash for the woods he could easily escape, he figured, but if he went back to help his partner, he had only half a chance. He gazed back again at Watson, still calling for him. Then ran back to help him.

"Get me up," shouted Watson.

"Take my hand!"

Watson did, and Porter pulled him over the fence. Watson crashed to the ground. Both men got to their feet and took off running.

CHAPTER 8

Porter and Watson neared the woods. They glanced behind and descried saw the mob 50 yards back, running faster than they, and closing.

The weeks of little food in captivity began to take its toll on Porter. His head began swimming. The treeline ahead lost focus. His pace slackened.

"Watson!. . ." he shouted.

He needed Watson's help but Watson kept running. He collapsed to one knee. He panted. Presently a half dozen men surrounded him. He stood to run but could barely walk. The remaining mob continued after Watson. Within a minute they caught him as well.

They grabbed both men and escorted them back to jail. Suddenly Watson was quickly diverted to the courthouse "secured room" to be held separately from Porter. Meanwhile, Porter could barely walk, so they practically drug him along. They shouted at him, and that began to anger him. They arrived in front of the building where a larger crowd was gathering. He slid out of their grasp, ran to the doorway, and faced the mob. A voice shouted, "Pass the rope."

A rope was passed over their heads and a new man grabbed him — but Porter pushed him into the mud. Porter noticed by the door a buckskin filled with lead musket balls. He grabbed it and shouted to the mob, "Stand back! "

They stopped and glared at him holding the weapon. Several of the mob drew out bowie knives and advanced.

Porter grabbed the Missourian in the mud by his hair, and swung the ammo bag ominously. "I'll crush his head and any others that takes another step at me."

They stopped again.

Sheriff Reynolds then stepped in front of the mob with his shotgun. The men with knives halted. Porter released his victim. The sheriff shouted, and pulled Porter inside.

There, Reynolds turned the shotgun on Porter, and descended with him to the basement cell.

"Where's Watson?" said Porter.

"He's being taken to St. Louis for trial. I reckon you won't see him again unless he happens to get buried in the same cemetery as you."

Porter was angry that Watson had talked him into the escape attempt. He figured Watson would never have attempted escaping alone, and had used Porter in the gamble. And now Porter's punishment would be even more severe.

He awakened the next morning, starved. He had been ironed with his right hand to his left foot — where he could not straighten his back. The door opened and the jailer walked in with a covered dish. He left it and slammed the iron grate behind him. Porter uncovered the dish to find a dead rat.

Twenty-four hours later the jailer entered, saw the rat, and left without a word. Downstairs, he reported to Reynolds the rat was uneaten. "And it's beginning to smell."

The following day, the jailer again entered, gave the rat a glance, and muttered, "Sheriff says you're only entitled to bread and water. I'm sorry, but meat dishes are no longer allowed."

Porter ignored his insipid humor, staring at the wall.

The jailer smiled, went inside, and took the rat out, replacing it with crusts of bread and water.

He noticed after 18 days that the pain in his wrists had disappeared entirely; the tight irons had loosened enough for him to slip them up to his elbows and turn his arms around inside them — he'd lost that much weight.

He picked a louse and flicked it. Others were embedded deeply in his eyebrows. His color was pale. His eyes were both green and red.

He was dying.

CHAPTER 9

In the late afternoon Porter heard his door swing open. In walked several officers, including one with his hand clutched to his pistol. They stood over him and stared.

Porter wondered if they were going to end his misery. One knelt and uncuffed him.

"Get up, boy, we're going for a ride," said the oldest, a tall, skinny deputy with a badge seemingly half the size of his chest.

"I ain't going till I wash up," said Porter.

"Well, that's your choice, but you better hurry. A mob's forming outside, and they got word we're moving you!"

"Where're we going?"

"You'll learn soon enough."

Downstairs, Porter quickly bathed, running a sponge from a bucket across his body in less than 30 seconds.

"Now get me a clean set of clothes," he said.

"Don't have time."

"You make time — or I ain't moving."

"What's your beef?" said the older deputy.

"My clothes have rotted."

"It's your neck," said the oldest. He disappeared, only to return five minutes later with clean clothes. "That mob is beginning to broil." He glanced to the other three deputies, who understood his look and in one motion pulled out revolvers.

"Hurry up," said the oldest officer to Porter. "We can't do much to protect you against a mob."

"Then hand me a couple of those guns," said Porter, "and I'll do it myself."

The officers were not amused by him. They shoved him out the door.

Outside, the officers held their guns on the mob, and in the last remaining rays of sunset tied Porter's feet under a dilapidated saddle and his hands behind his back. Two of the deputies led him off on a fast trot: the old, skinny one and the foppish-looking younger one, a lad of 19. The only distinguishing feature about either of them, Porter noted, was their identical handle-bar mustaches, caked with dried nasal fluid and food particles. Perhaps they were father and son, he mused.

"I hear talk," said the younger a mile later, "that some of the more adventurous souls back there plan to ambush us before we get to Liberty, maybe even before we get to the Missouri River."

"You believe every scuttlebutt rumor you hear?" said the older, noticeably nervous nevertheless.

"Sometimes I do," said the younger, "if it involves my neck."

The night fell and the sky was thick with stars. As they rode, Porter realized how easily they could be ambushed from the roadside. He could not actually see the trunks of trees, but was vaguely sensible of them against the darkness. Among them he imagined human figures.

A stranger's outline appeared directly in front of them. "Mind if I ride with you to the river?" He sat horseback, silhouetted against the stars.

"These woods are haunted," replied the younger deputy.

"But you can ride in front of us," said the older. "And let me have your gun."

The stranger hesitantly complied. He was an aged, wiry soul that resembled a gnarled old tree.

Night creatures were crying and warbling. Porter heard a distant owl.

None of the party said a word. Porter kept gaping at the stranger, wandering if he were one of the mob out to get him, and if so, if he sported a knife.

Six miles later they arrived at the river. They spotted on the opposite shore eight men riding off a ferry and taking into the woods.

When the ferry returned, Porter's entourage boarded it. The older officer asked the operator, "Where are those eight men going?"

"To hew timber."

"At midnight?"

No reply; it was obvious who the men were.

Across the river they landed. Porter kept a watchful eye amidst the barely discernable trees. Three miles into the woods he heard a crackle behind him. The younger officer turned. "What's that?"

"What's what?" said the older one.

"That."

"You're hearing things. There's nothing back there."

"Then you're deaf," said the younger. "I heard it. And it ain't wood being cut. I still haven't heard a saw put to a tree, and you know as well as me we would in this still air."

Suddenly they all heard it — the crackling of brush and leaves directly behind them.

The two officers cocked their weapons. The older one cleared his throat. "Move faster, boy; keep your eyes behind you."

Porter's eyes went wide. "Unloose my hands and give me a gun."

The two officers stared at him, considering his offer.

"Give him one," said the younger.

"No," said the older, "just keep a look-out."

They heard several horse neighs — then realized they were about to be ambushed. Porter looked sternly into the older deputy's face, "I said give me a pistol!"

CHAPTER 10

Eight horsemen advanced on them at a quick trot, now pulling out rifles.

The older deputy, riding at a near trot, turned to his prisoner. "Porter, you won't bolt if I give you one?"

Porter weighed the choice a moment, realizing he could
easily escape in the night if he were armed, but he also discerned the old gentleman expected an honest answer, so all he
could manage to say was, "I'll stay with you."

The older deputy threw Porter a pepper-shot revolver. He
caught it, checked its chambers to see if it were loaded, and
suddenly wheeled his horse around to face his ambushers, who
had now caught up to them and halted.

"I got a shot for each of you gentlemen," shouted Porter.

The two deputies were surprised at Porter's sudden halting in the road. The older deputy was particularly taken back
by Porter's unauthorized taking charge of the situation.

"You go back now, gentlemen, or die on the spot," Porter
continued, now aiming at the lead horseman. "It's your choice.

But you'll have one less tooth and one less brain. The tooth goes first in my line of fire. Then goes your brain. 'Wouldn't be a pretty sight."

He could feel their unease, as he could see merely the darkened shadowy outlines of his ambushers. He knew they were considering his threat, and it became clearer what they would do when he heard one mutter to their leader, "Rockwell ain't worth dying for."

The leader sat atop his horse for what seemed to the deputies an interminable minute, re-assessing the scene. Both the deputies and Porter could see the ambushers' outlines 10 feet before them as they faced them head on. Finally their leader barked, "Move back!"

Porter sighed. He glanced to the two deputies on either side of him.

Suddenly the lead ambusher whirled back, whipping his rifle towards Porter and firing. The shot zinged past his ear. Porter twirled atop his saddle and got off two quick shots. The lead horseman jolted back, hit in the shoulder, and somersaulted onto the ground. As two other horsemen reached down to help him, three others opened fire.

Porter fired once, hitting one in the arm, and the two deputies opened fire with their pepper revolvers. Since this style of weapon lacked precision, they misfired several shots, but two from each pistol did go off. While only one of their shots hit an ambusher, Porter fired thrice more and one shot went off. Another horseman was hit in the arm, causing him to scream. All but two of the remaining horsemen panicked and rode off. The last two begged Porter to not shoot — they were out of their saddles and still helping their leader back to his horse. Within seconds they were all three back in their saddles and trotting away, their leader groaning.

The two deputies and Porter were left in peace, and finally the two lawmen looked over at Porter and blew out a silent sigh. They watched the darkened riders disappear downroad. Porter tossed the older deputy his peppershot revolver and turned his horse around to resume the journey.

While riding slowly a few minutes, the older man thought thoroughly through his question, and finally spoke. "Where'd you learn to shoot like that?"

"County fairs."

"'Ever lost?"

"Nope."

The younger deputy studied him in silence.

"I reckon you wonder where you're going."

"It's crossed my mind."

"The jail at Liberty, Missouri."

Porter remembered Joseph Smith's six month incarceration in the dungeon there and wondered if, for once, he should have broken his promise and escaped the deputies. But he knew his pa would have kept his word, and by Rockwell family tradition, his word was his bond.

They rode into the darkness six more hours before stopping.

Just before dawn, in the cool of a summer breeze, they arrived at Liberty, Missouri. Immediately Porter was cast into the jail.

After gazing around the basement dungeon walls where only a single dim shaft of light penetrated from a trap door, he took out his gold watch and opened it. In the top lid on the inside was a small picture of an attractive woman.

He studied for fully an hour a small, sober picture of Luana Beebe Rockwell, and wondered if, by now, she had found another man.

CHAPTER 11

Ten days passed. Porter appeared before a new judge, Austin A. King. He was a short, dark-complexioned Missourian whose facial features resembled a mule. He thumbed through papers and spoke with a heavy accent.

"Mr. Rockwell, your court-appointed attorney is Mr. Alexander Doniphan. He has sought to change venue up here to my court where he figured the jurors would have less prejudice. I've got news for him. These papers of Mr. Doniphan are too informal, the style is too casual, and I cannot consider this case. You've gotta return to Independence."

Porter simply stood there, taking the blow, suspecting a plan to keep him in custody forever. Maybe Watson was right.

As he and the two officers mounted up to return to Independence, he overheard the older officer mutter to the other, "We'll take a different road."

"The first one's shorter."

"I overheard more talk in the tavern," said the older. "Some folk plan to waylay him . . . I reckon somebody knew the judge's plan . . . I don't know how."

The two officers glanced at each other and both knew what the other was thinking . . . the honorable Judge King was not as honorable as some supposed.

By taking a little-traveled road, Porter and the two deputies rode three hours without seeing anyone. All three kept a watchful vigilance on the sides of the road in case additional ambushers lay in waiting.

At sundown they passed a wagon driven by an old man. He greeted the three cheerfully, and did not seem to be aware of Porter's notoriety. They all rode together in the moonlight. Several hours later they arrived back at Independence with no further encounters. As Porter parted with the two deputies, he turned to the younger one.

"What you read in the papers ain't necessarily the truth."

He studied both men and they nodded back.

At Independence jail again, Porter was immediately ironed hand and foot. He remained in the dungeon without use of his hands, only able to eat by leaning on his side and chewing his food off the floor like a dog.

A week later Reynolds replaced Porter's algae-infested water bowl with fresh water. Then placed an anxious eye on him. He noted Porter's hair growing outrageously long, greasy and itching from the increasing number of infesting lice.

Porter knew the sheriff had something on his mind, mainly from the manner in which he attempted to keep his voice casual, but the attempt was apparent.

"We've got a letter written by Joe Smith," said Reynolds, "and it shows his complete confidence in you. We're giving you a once-in-a-lifetime opportunity here, boy. You get Holy Joe into Missouri, get him into our hands, and we'll pay you any pile you name. You'll never suffer for want again, lad; that, I promise."

Porter said nothing.

Reynolds cleared his throat. "Am I clear?"

Porter blinked, half-conscious.

"I said — " continued Reynolds.

"I heard what you said."

"Well?"

"I'll see you damned first, and then I won't."

"All right, you'll wish you was never born."

Reynolds' fat face smirked.

And then Porter spat in it.

Reynolds wiped the spit from his cheek and forced a smile. And then left.

Upstairs, Reynolds nodded to three men in his office, and they descended to the dungeon. From his desk Reynolds heard muffled groans and smacking of fists, and the sound of boots on flesh. Reynolds leaned back in his chair and lifted his feet to his desk to read the newspaper.

CHAPTER 12

The following dawn the door crashed open. Porter jerked awake with a start and saw Sheriff Reynolds in the framework. Reynolds strutted up to him, stood silently over him, and stared down. Porter glanced at the sheriff's freshly polished boots. His stomach was too sore to take more punishment by kicking; he forced the thought from his mind and gazed directly into Reynolds' eyes.

Reynolds flushed with anger. He knelt to one knee, reached his right hand to his own belt, and pulled out a key. He unlocked the iron hobbles.

Outside, Porter was taken by the same two officers as earlier, who had just returned from another trip. When they saw his bruises, the older deputy chewed out Reynolds.

Porter felt relieved to be leaving the sheriff, and he wondered if his transfer were permanent.

Sheriff Reynolds scowled as the two deputies led his prisoner away. After failing in his plot to capture Joseph, Reynolds was now doubly angry Porter was being taken right out of his grasp. Outside on horseback, Porter heard the sheriff inside kicking the office wall. He smiled. As did the older deputy.

Riding out of town with the two lawmen, Porter noticed autumn leaves had faded to a dark, lifeless brown. The chill wind caught his face by surprise. He wondered if at the next stop he would again be hobbled in irons. He noted the old deputy staring at him often and apparently anxious to make Porter's trip bearable.

"Put this blanket over your shoulders, boy." After an hour the older officer spoke again. "You know, since we saw you, we've heard even more tales about you and your ways. 'It true you ran out all the thieves in Nauvoo?"

"All but myself," smiled Porter.

The older fellow nervously pulled some dried nasal discharge from his huge moustache and flicked it on the ground. "That's some renegade posse you ran there, I heard."

"Yep."

Both deputies, remembering Porter's fearless stand against the ambushers, had obviously been talking since last seeing him about the potential danger of transporting their prisoner if he got the mind to escape.

"Some folks say you about licked half the militia force at Crooked River yourself," continued the older one, still flicking.

"They deserved it," said Porter.

"I heartily agree," said the deputy.

Porter smiled, then looked at him. "Are you scared of me?"

The younger one got serious, "That thing at Crooked River. The militia had no right to plan an execution on them two Mormon prisoners. I'm glad you whupped 'em."

Porter nodded, appreciating their sincerity but amused by their apprehension.

"So how many county fairs have you won?" said the older.

"Lost count."

His escorts seemed anxious to deliver him quickly.

By the time he reached Liberty, Missouri his groin and thighs were raw from the rough, creaking saddle. Even his horse seemed anxious to unload him. It was the first time he could ever remember not riding in harmony with an animal.

At Liberty he was thrust into the dungeon again. He found it far worse than Independence.

To his dismay his hands were again ironed. Fortunately, however, the irons were not tight and his hands were placed in front of him. He was also finally able, to some extent, to use them.

But the next day he was dismayed to see the jailer from Independence arrive, yet felt fortunate it was not Sheriff Reynolds. For some reason it had been arranged to have his old jailer take over duties of looking after him, something that had been worked out between the two county sheriffs, he surmised. Perhaps in another effort to coerce him to betray Joseph. Porter felt less hopeful than ever he'd ever see daylight.

But on the second day, when his eyes caught hold of a stove pipe hole nine feet above the floor, his eyes brightened for the first time in months.

He finally knew he had a legitimate chance to escape . . .

CHAPTER 13

When the jailer left the building for the night, Porter removed the stove pipe with his shackled hands. He stared at the narrow tunnel and figured he would never be able to fit through it. Additionally, his body still ached from bruises. However, he stripped himself of his clothes and pushed them through the stove pipe hole, then slithered inside. He was finally able to pull himself up, with his hands still cuffed, to the ceiling space above. There, he began crawling between the basement ceiling and the floor of the first story.

Crawling in this space was difficult: His naked wounds were scratched, and he bled. In the darkness he felt spider webs and assorted insects crawling across him. He saw a set of green eyes in the dark, and knew it was a rat, just inches from his nose. It was staring at him. He wondered if it wished to feed on his wounds. He spat at the animal and it turned away.

He finally found loose boarding above his head. With the soft end of his fist he smashed a floorboard upward.

Light filtered through. He smashed another floorboard. He crawled up to the floor of the first story and stood.

When he shuffled to the first, inner door that led outside he found it bolted shut. The windows were also barred. There was no way out. The first floor itself was a prison, he figured, yet he would just have to think through a plan of escape.

Back to his cell he crawled, replacing the loose floorboards. He had left no clues for the jailer to discover he had escaped to the first floor and returned to his dungeon.

All the following day he agonized over how he could get past that locked door. His old jailer entered with the evening "meal," consisting of cabbage soup. It was water and one cabbage leaf the size of a small coin. The jailer knelt beside him, regarding him.

Porter wondered if he had somehow figured out the escape attempt — if he had left loose boards above.

"I reckon," said the jailer, scratching his half-bald head with long skinny fingers, "if you realize how much better life would be if you didn't try to escape."

Porter's eyes darted about. He was not certain his attempt had been discovered, but he wanted to know for certain. He glanced at the jailer. "Who'd want to escape?"

The jailer smiled. "That's what I figured. You learned your lesson at Independence when you escaped from me, didn't you? Ain't it easier to just let things be?"

Porter studied him, relieved to know no one was the wiser.

At the Hamilton House in Carthage was a favorite watering hole for many in Hancock County. It was known to many as Hamilton Tavern although it was actually a hotel that contained a tavern. Tonight, Porter sat, swishing whiskey around his teeth before swallowing it. He had just gone from the river shore to visiting his mother in Nauvoo, whereupon he had decided to take a ride in the country, and had wound up here.

Upon seeing his ma, he was touched when she smiled at the door. He thanked her for bringing the attorney fees to Missouri, and hugged her tearfully. He was also moved in a nostalgic sort of way when his old dog greeted him. The dog was a strange mixture, with the ears of a dachshund, the nose of a boxer, the body of a St. Bernard, and the tail of a dinosaur — it was simply huge; its fur was curly like a poodle's but black. It was remarkably ugly. Hence its name — Ugly. Many people laughed when they looked at the thing, but Porter had loved it since a puppy. It had moved with him three times in Missouri and twice in Illinois as his people had been driven, and for years it had never left his side. Now he was back. He petted the creature and it rolled on its back. It yelped and danced around, leaping on him and nearly knocking him over. It ran through the yard, and Porter and his mother laughed. His wife had liked its companionship for the children but had found it too expensive to feed and, if the truth be known, among other reasons, she really had found it becoming too eccentric and bothersome; for example, it had developed the disconcerting habit of barking at the moon whenever the moon was full. Porter's mother in fact now often used it as a calendar for that very purpose. Sarah Rockwell therefore had kept the animal since Porter had given it to her at Luana's insistence before his exile East.

She also had some advice for her son. She encouraged him to stay close to Emily. She reported that his younger children had adjusted well to his departure the last year — due primarily to their young age and to his not being around that much anyway before his trip East — but that Emily still held him in her heart closer than anyone. After an hour Porter departed with his dog.

Now, inside the tavern, Ugly sat beside him and watched him sip his whiskey. Porter was desperate for employment, and crushed over his family. He gave the dog a shot of whiskey. Ugly shook his head and sneezed.

Porter saw himself in the saloon mirror. He was a scrawny sight compared to his former self, but he would rebuild his muscles, he determined, and would yet be of value to Joseph.

Three tables away in the soft tavern light, Porter vaguely discerned the faces of the Higbee brothers, along with William

Law, one of the highest ranking Mormons, a member of Joseph's First Presidency. Though Porter did not know them well enough, he had occasionally doubted their loyalty to Joseph, and his suspicions were confirmed, of course, by Watson.

He wondered why the men there engaged in such soft discourse. He lowered his head in order to not be seen. Certainly his hair and beard provided an elaborate disguise, although Higbee had likely heard the news of Porter's strange return to Joseph's party, complete with long hair and beard. The men did not take notice of him nor anyone else in the busy tavern, so enthralled were they in their discussion. The room was noisy, and Porter could only catch snatches of their conversation. He picked up that they were planning some sort of newspaper enterprise. He then overheard something that — although he could not make out full details of it — enabled him to finally comprehend their business: the overthrow of Joseph's city!

Suddenly he noticed another face — one he had never seen but of which he quickly learned the identity — Thomas Sharp, a man who had taken upon himself the mantle of fighting the growing Mormon political power in Hancock County and throughout the state under the masthead of his own newspaper, the *Warsaw Signal,* as well as under the banner of the Anti-Mormon Party, known to most as the "Anties," which he had founded in 1841. Sharp's newspaper was published in nearby Warsaw and read by most non-Mormons in Carthage and the surrounding cities of Nauvoo. Sharp was considered a powerful figure.

Porter rose casually and strode to the door. A glance back from the doorway allowed him to catch a suspicious, kerosene

lamp-reflected glint in one eye of Chauncey Higbee taking notice of him.

He studied Porter's face.

Porter quickly turned, pulled his hat low, and walked into
the cold.

His dog followed.

Porter rode in a flash. He was two miles outside Carthage
when he heard horsehooves pounding behind. At first he figured riders were merely traveling to Nauvoo . . . until he realized . . . they were after him!

His horse tired. It slowed.

His pursuers gained on him.

He managed to return it to a gallop. The horsemen were a
hundred yards back now and closing.

Then his horse lost a shoe.

CHAPTER 24

Porter jumped from his horse and ran to the cover of thick brush. Through the woods he could hear the horsemen advancing, and soon they trotted on either side of him, not seeing his humped figure concealed in the brush.

He took off running to his left. His feet were still sore from his Missouri trek, but the boots allowed him substantial protection. He heard horses just out of sight. He jumped behind a fallen tree and crawled to one end. His dog followed silently. Slipping inside the log, he pulled his dog in beside him. Then he noticed Ugly's tail wagging outside the log. He pulled him in even closer.

He could see his pursuers stopping and scanning the woodland. Slowly they advanced. He wondered if they had spotted the dog.

They disappeared from his view a moment, then he heard them leap over the log and begin to gallop.

He sighed with relief. He heard the horsemen scattering in the distance, swearing and shouting questions at each other.

Suddenly he noticed beside him — rather, he smelled beside him — a pungent odor . . . and quickly realized . . . it was a skunk.

A live skunk.

He strained his eyes outside the log for other cover but saw none. He glanced back at the skunk. The animal's shining eyes regarded him, then his dog, then waddled away to the other end of the log. Porter struggled to keep his dog still. His heart pounded, hoping Ugly would not rile up the creature. Even with his dog's reputation for ripe woodland scents, he hoped a skunk would not be part of his portfolio. His mind quickly scanned across the years, trying to recall even once when Ugly had returned with skunk scent; relieved, he could not remember any. But then, there's always a first time . . .

Porter waited with baited breath . . .

Ugly stayed still and quiet.

Porter knew that even if the dog had been attracted to the creature, perhaps he was respectfully retaining his distance in order to protect his master. Then again, Porter thought, with an animal of Ugly's sense of the absurd, Porter was in the most vulnerable position ever in their several year history for what could be the decade's cruelest practical joke . . .

Nevertheless Ugly continued to remain still.

Porter sighed with relief. He heard two more horses pass over him, while others passed around the log.

The last horseman passed just as the skunk exited. A horse hoof caught the skunk by surprise, and the small, striped animal reared its tail.

The other horsemen ahead heard a simultaneous horse whinny and human scream. Presently, a horse passed them riderless in a thunderous gallop.

THE PORTER ROCKWELL CHRONICLES

All the mob horsemen, curious, came to a halt and trotted back. They found their comrade on the ground, sitting upright, steaming with anger. They all burst into laughter. He was drenched in skunk scent.

Porter and his dog meanwhile ran on foot behind the cover of thick trees, fully a quarter mile away, directly towards Nauvoo . . . chuckling softly.

Porter and Ugly arrived at Joseph's home and rushed into his study. Porter told him all he had seen at the tavern. Joseph pondered a moment, and turned to him:

"When I travel, will you again be my bodyguard?"

"Of course," said Porter.

"And I'll convert the front room into a tavern so you can have regular employment."

Moments later the two men sat, eating cake.

"How long has he been with her?" said Porter.

Joseph, somewhat surprised by Porter's directness, studied him a moment, then answered:

"They've been courting a half year now; he's quite proper about it and I believe he is a good man."

"I always thought him a fool."

"It's easy to be bitter."

"Those are my young ones he's influencing."

Joseph nodded.

"I don't know what to do," said Porter.

"There's not a lot you can."

"She might break up with him if I tried seein' her more."

"And she might not — unless you give it time."

"Time for her to take him for good?"

"Time for the resentment to heal."

Porter returned Ugly to his ma's, where the animal would remain, being pampered like royalty by a doting, loving older lady. On occasion Ugly would wander to the Mansion House to visit Porter, and at Joseph's insistence Emma would let him in, much to her dismay.

Porter caught the subtle conflicts between Joseph and Emma over his animal and it made him smile. Emma was gracious enough to not argue over a close friend's pet, yet held serious reservations about the beast. So, her innuendos were never-ceasing and ever-amusing to both men.

When she left for a furniture-buying excursion in St. Louis, Joseph had Porter's bar quickly constructed in a front room.

Within hours it had a decent clientele. Both men wondered how Emma would take to the concept. "It may be too late for her to do anything about it," said Joseph. "At least that's my thinking on the matter."

Emma would be returning that evening.

"We'll find out soon enough," added Porter.

Although Joseph had intended for the Mansion House to be shared with one and all and to serve everyone within its capacity to serve, Emma did not exactly share his fraternal views. True, she allowed his vision to incorporate usage of the house as a meeting place for church and civic councils, and as a hotel, and she even allowed him to procure needed cash from it by leasing the building to one Ebenezer Robinson, beginning that very month for $1,000 per year while maintaining only several rooms for the Smith family. But upon returning home from St. Louis that night she was shocked to find in her front room the hastily but elaborately constructed tavern.

She tromped upstairs to Joseph's study and confronted him.

"I'm obligated to Porter," Joseph explained. "And this will give him regular employment."

"And I'm obligated to the children," said Emma. "I will not have them raised under such conditions nor have them mingle with men who frequent such a place. You are at liberty to make your choice; either that bar goes, or we will."

CHAPTER 25

That evening Joseph told Porter her ultimatum: "You can take your meals with us a few months. And stay with us till you find employment. But the bar goes."

Porter noticed his sheepishness, and both men chuckled.

Emma truly did not mind Porter's staying, although she was not particularly fond of his roughness.

Joseph then reiterated to him that he wished to keep him nearby for his personal defense.

"As long as we keep that dog's visits to a minimum," later added Emma, "I suppose it's all right."

Porter still managed to bring the dog's strange scents into her home, however; so Porter was, in her mind, still not entirely welcome. Porter managed after all these years to wash the animal after Ugly's occasional excursions into odiferous realms, but the odors always lingered with both individuals.

Porter was grateful for Emma's kindnesses to him, with or without Ugly.

He did not know for certain, but he sensed Joseph still did not fully believe his story about the plot on his life. He made a comment to that effect and Joseph looked down, saying nothing. Frustrated, he retired upstairs to wash, and came up with a strategy: As Joseph's bodyguard he would carry two loaded pistols and 50 rounds of ammo at all times, plus a pair of dueling pistols concealed in his clothing. He felt complete confidence in his ability to protect Joseph. He planned to target practice each day again, work hard in Joseph's corral, eat heartily, and regain his bear-like form. He would see his dog every few days when he'd visit his mother and siblings at her home, and would try to remain balanced and busy, and keep in touch with all his family, but the events about to be thrust upon him kept him too busy to visit with anyone for more than a few minutes. The same was true for his visits even with Emily. Luana had mellowed since his first returning from jail, and although she would not see Porter herself, she conveyed messages through Cutler. She now allowed Porter to visit Emily as often as he liked, and even take her with him if he wished. So he saw her almost daily. But the other children were satisfied to only see him Saturdays; thereupon he would usually take them to the river to play.

He observed during this period that the youngest three had a life of their own. They seemed to enjoy his company but did not crave it, as Emily did. They were in fact closer to their mama, as they had always been. Meanwhile, Emily and her mother did not get along so well.

She was indeed "Papa's little girl." And she was 14 now.

"Why don't you get along better with your mama?" Porter asked her on one occasion.

"You have to ask me?" she replied.

Porter smiled. "It's that bad, huh?"

"It's gotten worse the last year while you were gone. And now she takes out everything on me instead of you. But if I stand up to her . . . well, you know how she gets. So I don't stand up to her."

"Are you scared of her?"

"I have nothing to be scared of if I always give in to her. So that's what happens. And then we get along fine."

Porter seethed underneath. He wished he were home in the thick of the battle with Luana so Emily could be free to think — or at least express herself — as she wished, without being overpowered.

"I thought I loved her and missed her while I was back East and in jail. I guess I did. Now I just wish she'd be good to you."

"But you still want her back, don't you, Papa?"

Porter thought a moment. He really did, despite her difficult ways.

He nodded.

And she smiled at him.

A knock came at the Mansion House. Joseph rarely answered the door himself for safety reasons, but on this occasion did, and saw two teenage lads standing there awkwardly.

"Come in."

The two were Dennison L. Harris and Robert Scott, the latter living as a border with the William Law family. The two entered and Porter joined tham from the kitchen. The two boys took a seat at Joseph's request and got right to business. They apprised Joseph of a secret movement to take his life.

Joseph felt the air knocked out of him, realizing it was connected to Porter's information. And he was not yet ready to accept the facts of such a betrayal.

"By whom?" he finally said.

"Men who you probably think are your close friends," said young Harris.

Joseph glanced over at Porter.

"We were invited to meetings by Mr. Law," said young Robert Scott. "William Law. He is one of the group's leaders."

William Law was also one of Joseph's two trusted counselors in the church's First Presidency. His brother Wilson Law was also a part of the group.

Not mentioned or proven as one of the conspirators however was a man whom Joseph would later learn was a traitor to him, and who would be dropped from the church high council and would eventually on his own accord leave Nauvoo — William Marks. Marks lived but a block and a half west of Joseph. He was more than a neighbor, he was president of the Nauvoo Stake.

Joseph's dissidents came in varying shades, the darkest of which proved to be conspirers against his life, most of whom from a core who would start their own church on April 28, 1844. The president of this church was William Law.

While Marks was plotting behind Joseph's back on other matters traitorous to Joseph, he was not a member of the constituency plotting against his life.

Particularly saddening to Joseph was the fact both Marks and Law had participated in "anointing and ordaining" Joseph to the "highest and holiest order of the priesthood" just four months previously, September 28, 1843. Porter sensed his friend feeling more pity for the two men than for himself. Joseph reflected only a few moments before turning to the two lads.

"I suggest you go to them," said Joseph, "but take no part in the proceedings, and report back to me."

Joseph thanked them and they left. Joseph stared at Porter as if in a daze. Porter felt at once relieved that Joseph was finally convinced of his danger, and sorry for him, knowing that the reality of the betrayal had finally hit home. Tears welled up in Porter's eyes; he felt he knew a little something about betrayal also.

Porter lay in bed, unable to sleep. Thoughts of his children and Luana haunted him. He opened his pocketwatch and gazed at her picture inside. He wondered if she and Cutler would marry and if her new husband's affections would be as his own — if Luana had a man who really loved her. He snapped the watch shut and returned it to his pocket. After he petted his dog beside the bed a moment, he arose. Then shuffled to the window and stared at the moon. He realized he could not endure the uncertainty, knowing that in later years he might kick himself for not even trying when he had the chance. He slipped on his trousers and boots, and set off to see Luana.

Due to Porter's obligations to protect Joseph in recent evenings, it had been three days since Emily had seen her pa. She was inside cooking a late meal, missing her father to the point of pain.

Porter approached the massive door he had built.

He glanced at the window and perceived a pair of eyes watching. He looked closer and espied the eyes as intense as he had always known them. They were the eyes he had never been able to release from his mind. He wondered if she were feeling even a particle of what he felt.

Luana disappeared from the glass window.

Porter stopped at the front door. There, he tapped gently. The door was opened. Emily greeted him with a huge hug and a loud exclamation of, "Papa!" Then excused herself to pick up the other children from a neighbor's party several blocks away.

Luana stared at Porter as he strode inside to the fireplace, picked up a rod, and began jabbing hot embers. He shifted from one foot to the other. He suspected that any recalling of fond memories he might bring up could backfire — she could counter it with negative memories of anything he might say — so he said nothing. He became aware that the dominant sound in the room was a loud wall clock.

She finally broke the awkward silence. "What do you want?"

CHAPTER 26

Porter just studied Luana. He felt unexpected feelings rippling back like rings in a river after a rock was thrown. "Thanks for letting me see Emily so much. "It'd be nicer if you were part of the deal."

She gave him a long, searching look. "We've been through this. You had your chance for a decade."

"I want it back."

"'Too late."

"Who says?"

"Me," came Cutler's voice as he entered from the kitchen. "Can't you see she wishes to be left alone?"

Porter was surprised Cutler was even present. His horse must have been hitched at the rear of the house. Porter decided to diffuse the man's anger. He stepped forward and attempted to shake his hand.

Cutler eased his emotions and returned the handshake.

"Sorry to bother you, Alpheas, I just wanted a little talk with her if you don't mind, then I'll be on my way."

Despite Porter's amiability, Cutler nevertheless refused to leave the room. So Porter ignored him and finally shoved the rod back into the embers.

"Luana," said Porter, "What do you really want from me?"

"Just what Alpheas said."

"These embers could be rekindled."

Luana stared at him.

Cutler spoke up again. "Porter, I really think it would be best if you leave now."

Porter ignored him and kept his gaze on her. Luana placed her hand on Cutler's shoulder.

"Porter," she said, "The embers have died, and everything's been said."

"Except one thing." And then he paused.

"Well?"

"What I feel."

She gazed at him coldly.

"Luana," Porter began. "I want you to know. . ." But he could not finish. He could see everything in her eyes. Everything that was dead. He sighed, turned and walked away.

At Joseph's home, the two lads, Harris and Scott, reported on three meetings they had attended with William Law. They gave him details about a conspiracy whose members consisted of Chauncey Higbee, Francis Higbee, Joseph Jackson, William Law, Jane Law, Wilson Law, Robert Foster, Charles Foster, Henry Norton, John Hicks, Charles Ivins, and Augustin Spencer to assassinate him and take control of the church and the city. Joseph was surprised about who all comprised the conspiracy beyond the Law brothers. He had to fight through his emotions in 10 minutes of silence, recalling briefly his history with each of the dozen souls. At the end of his reverie he shook his head.

Then he turned to Porter and uttered, "Now it's time to defend ourselves."

On March 24, 1844 Joseph publicly indicted Chauncey L. Higbee as plotting against his life. He also excommunicated Wilson and William Law and the latter's wife, Jane, and on April 13th he arrested Robert D. Foster for slander and for conspiracy against his life.

Soon thereafter was a pounding at the door of the Mansion House. Porter answered it to discover the Nauvoo city marshal, Thomas Greene, a lanky, likeable, but officious sort, holding a prisoner, Augustin Spencer, one of the alleged conspirators. Spencer was short, young, intelligent, and well-cultivated.

"What's the trouble?" said Joseph, coming to the door.

"He's the trouble," said Spencer, nodding at the marshal, who held Spencer in a tight grip.

"Joseph," said Marshal Greene, "I'm taking Spencer to my office to book charges. He just attacked his own brother with his fists — and I saw it. But first he wanted to talk to you."

Augustin Spencer struggled to free himself of Greene's hold. "Joseph, I'll prepare a lawsuit against the both of you if you don't order him to let go of me."

Since Joseph was the mayor of Nauvoo, and the Mansion House was used as the city building for both the mayor's and the marshal's office, Joseph unavoidably saw most of the trouble that occurred in the city. He wished at times he weren't quite so entrenched in civic duties, taking upon himself the praesidia of community leadership, but most of the other men in the church with like multi-faceted abilities happened to be overseas: Brigham Young was his senior member of the Council of the Twelve and was in the Eastern U.S. performing missionary work, as were most of the Quorum of the Twelve. They were needed there to convert others, Joseph felt, and export their harvests to Nauvoo to expand the size and strength of the church. Therefore, Joseph accepted the fact that he was thus faced with more responsibilities than he cared to face, and today was a typical example. Brigham in fact would be just such the man to handle such a problem as this, he mused.

At the door Porter noticed several others arriving, shouting at Marshal Greene and calling for Greene and Joseph to release Spencer. Immediately Porter recognized all eight — they were the conspirators! William Law, characteristically, was at the back of the group attempting to restrain the heated anger of the rest. Everything he tried, however, failed, as his associates only escalated their emotions when they beheld Joseph's firmness. William Law then attempted to reason with Joseph: He claimed the Spencer brothers always had their little rows and that they themselves would settle it. Marshal Greene was simply overreacting.

Joseph refused his request.

Then, one of their group, Charles Foster, began swearing, and drew a revolver from his vest to shoot Joseph. Porter spotted it and launched forward. He wrestled the weapon away and clenched Foster's neck in a vice-like hold.

Joseph immediately ordered Greene and Porter to bring in the two violent prisoners to be fined. He ordered the others to immediately disperse. They strode away, livid with rage, especially William Law, who departed with a passion pounding in his heart — that Joseph as usual would not follow his advice. Certainly Law was better suited to run the city and the church than he, and certainly his plans for the overthrow — for a complete revolution — were justified. And in his mind it could not come soon enough.

CHAPTER 27

Hancock County had been organized 15 years earlier. And Carthage was now not only the center of county court activity but was the nearest substantial non-Mormon town, 12 miles southeast of Nauvoo.

Here, the conspirators launched an attack against Joseph on the legal battlefield; they took their story of the arrest to a Carthage grand jury. At this court they claimed Spencer and Foster had been falsely arrested by Joseph.

Not only from this legal case, but from other reports by dissident Mormons beginning primarily with the John C. Bennett incident two years earlier, the Carthaginians were becoming increasingly concerned about their Mormon neighbors. The Mormon topic in fact was now beginning to consume their conversation on every street corner and in every store.

Joseph decided to plead his case to the Carthage grand jury. He enlisted Hyrum Smith, his brother, John Taylor, Porter Rockwell, and several others to accompany him to Carthage. Hyrum Smith and John Taylor both were tall, spare, grave, and dignified; they were men of thick brown hair and thoughtful demeanor. Both were in their late thirties, likeable, and undeniably loyal to Joseph.

At the courtroom Joseph demanded to the judge, "Please investigate the charges."

"I'm sorry, I'll have to delay action on the case until next term, but your case will be heard fairly." That one delaying action alone set up enough time to allow an avalanche of events to pour down on Joseph.

As he and his friends left the court, Joseph turned to Porter:

"Just this week I've learned about Joseph Jackson among the conspirators. He's committed murder, robbery, and perjury, and I can prove it by half-a-dozen witnesses. But the recent rumors he has created will fly against us now and we can't even defend ourselves by proving our innocence."

Porter felt anger at the court delays, as well.

Upon leaving the courthouse, they stopped at the Hamilton House tavern in Carthage. Inside, Joseph spotted Chauncey Higbee, one of the conspirators, seated at a large table.

Higbee, who was 40, muscular and tall, had in earlier years been considered somewhat of a street ruffian, but more recently had become self-educated, had befriended the intelligentsia of the church, and had even learned to display some restraint in his well-publicized temper.

Therefore, Porter was surprised when Higbee spotted them and raised his voice:

"No need for us to read river pirate stories in the newspapers anymore, Joseph. Folks say we've got our own pirates now, and they've taken over the county."

The crowd turned quiet. Joseph gazed at Higbee and said nothing; he sensed Higbee's courage was coming from his liquor.

Higbee became louder. "And some hide behind their long-haired animals." Higbee glared at Porter.

Porter piped in, "Some oughta be grateful the animals don't bite back."

Higbee got louder. "Well, Porter, if the folks knew how much the pirates stole from them they'd dump them in the Mississippi. And then we'd all be free from the river rats."

"Higbee," said Porter softly, "Joseph's done more in one week for the downtrodden in these parts than you and all your ilk could do in a lifetime. And he hasn't taken one cent for himself."

"Well," said Higbee, louder, "most pirates have only visions of power and greed. A really good one has that plus the wool pulled over the politicians' faces. I'm afraid your friend is a really good one."

Porter walked up to Higbee, reached a hand to his lapel, and grabbed it.

Higbee found himself being pulled from a sitting to a standing position, being stretched up against the wall. His face suddenly shone with sweat.

Porter gazed into his large, liquid eyes, and his voice quaked.

"Apologize to Joseph, Higbee."

CHAPTER 28

Higbee's face began to discompose. He was embarrassed that a man considerably shorter than himself had him so intimidated.

Then Porter felt a cold piece of metal stuck against his neck. He slowly turned to see the inn-keeper, Artois Hamilton, leveling a shot-gun against his skin.

"You fire that thing," said Porter, "with that barrel plugged up against me, and it just might back-fire." He turned and glared into Hamilton's eyes.

Hamilton smiled, "Then again, it might not."

Joseph broke the tense silence. "Porter, I think we're finished here."

Hamilton cleared his throat, "Yeah, I think you are."

Porter nodded a sardonic farewell to the men in the tavern, and clopped across the wooden floor in his boots and out the door.

Joseph sighed, relieved, and followed. He glanced at Higbee and saw hatred like he'd rarely seen. Higbee's long, horse-like face grew red. He spoke up just as Joseph reached the door.

"All pirates eventually see their empires crumble, Joseph. Just like Laffitte at Campeche, my friend."

Days later in Nauvoo, on June 7, 1844, Chauncey Higbee peered admirably at his work of art. The first issues of the *Nauvoo Expositor* flapped off the press in its own two-story brick building on the north side of Mulholland between Bluff and Page streets, and before the ink was dry he was grabbing a bundle, smelling the crisp fresh paper and taking it proudly outside.

Onto busy Mulholland Street he raced, handing out one issue after another, determined not only for every citizen in Nauvoo to receive a copy, but for every person in three counties to read it.

Higbee moved westward toward the temple with his pile of papers, and after he had walked one block he strode across the street into the Amos Davis Store and Hotel, where he disappeared.

Since it was Saturday, and with Luana gone, Porter visited his children the entire morning at Luana's home. At noon Cutler returned to the house. Porter told him he was taking Emily to accompany him into the commercial district. Cutler argued but Porter ignored him and left with her.

"He sure likes to boss you, huh?" mumbled Porter to her outside.

She smiled and nodded.

Near the temple Porter noticed Higbee exiting from the Amos Davis Store and Hotel across the street. Higbee spotted him and stared at the back of his head. Porter felt the stare and turned. Their eyes met and held. Higbee winced.

Intimidated, Higbee disappeared back inside the store. Porter forced away his anger and resumed riding up Mulholland with Emily. He observed myriads of citizens standing along the street, each reading a newspaper. He finally overheard several mumble:

"This could start a war if outsiders believe it."

"What's it say?"

"'Says Joseph is a tyrant and a thief.'"

When Porter and Emily arrived at the Mansion House with a copy of the paper to show Joseph, they found him already reading it, alongside Hyrum.

"What are we going to do about it?" said Porter.

Joseph and Hyrum just looked at him.

Porter noticed the sun getting low and decided to take Emily home. Smelling trouble in the air, he was anxious to return quickly to Joseph.

As he rode through town with Emily he observed citizens moving uneasily about — with quick movements — nervous perhaps. He wondered what the reaction would be in surrounding non-Mormon towns. He visualized what he had witnessed in Missouri thrice before — concerned citizens demanding their removal. As he brought Emily home he found Luana alone, surprised to see him. The children were napping and Cutler was away at work. Emily left her parents to be alone, hoping — praying — some reconciliation might occur.

Luana's mouth trembled. "I thought you weren't coming back with her till dark."

"I changed my mind."

CHAPTER 29

"We can't keep changing our minds."

"I can if I have to."

"You have to play by the rules, if you play at all, Porter. I don't want you visiting me — just the children."

He looked her over and blew out a silent sigh.

"I didn't plan to see you, but I can't give up this easy," he said.

She just stared at him.

"You like this Cutler fellow that much, huh?"

"We're getting married."

Porter was surprised it had really gone this far. "Maybe you don't know him well enough."

"I know I want him."

Porter sighed silently again. "We're a family, Luana."

"Was a family. Joseph is your family now. Luana unveiled quietly her own pent-up anger. "You still spend all your time with him?"

"He needs me."

"'Always has."

"Now especially," he said, "what with things the way they are."

"Things?"

"Tensions."

"There have always been tensions."

"Not like this," he said. "Outsiders lust after our property. Things are a lot different."

"I guess a lot of things are different."

He understood what she meant and it angered him:

"You really think I'll let you go through this thing with Cutler?"

"Do you really think you can stop it?"

"I can fight it."

"To what avail?"

"I can fight him."

"And what would that serve?"

"The children need me back. I'm their father."

"Physically only."

"Eternally."

"Alpheas and I are having the children sealed to us," she said. Porter felt his breath fall out of him. It was the belief of Mormons that marriage in their temple could be performed not just for this life but for the hereafter. "Sealing" was the term used for both marriages and ordinances to link children with their parents for the hereafter. Porter sickened at the prospect of losing his children even for this life.

"The devil you are," he said. "They ain't being sealed to nobody else."

"You gave up that privilege long ago."

"Who says?"

"The divorce decree says," she answered. "I'm free now and so are they."

"Ask them who they want as their father. They can't be sealed to anybody without *their* say."

"They're too young. I speak for them — and we divorced you, Porter."

"It was a piece of paper!"

"A paper that's binding," she said.

"They can't be sealed to Cutler!"

"Leave the house!"

"When I'm finished!"

"Can't you see — we are!"

"Ask them!" he said. "See what they think — see what they wanna do!"

"Porter, the issue is dead!"

"Ask them!"

"Do you want me to call the marshal?"

"Answer my question!" he shouted.

"I've answered it! We're all free from you — no matter who they want — they go with me! Is that clear!"

"Who are you to decide for them!" he said.

"Their legal parent! I have the right to decide for them!"

"You've taken away their choice to choose!" he said. "What's fair about that?"

"Nobody said it was fair! But that's where the court ruled. And the court's gotta start somewhere. Usually it's here — with their mama — 'cause you menfolk are supposed to be too busy out earning a living. But you were just too busy and out, period."

Porter sighed and lowered his voice. He walked to the fireplace, sat, and stared at the darkened ashes. "But I wouldn't be away ever again."

She also calmed. "I heard that five years ago."

"It was you who got rid of me two years ago," he said, louder.

"And where were you five years ago? You chose to stay away from us day after day and come home only on weekends half our marriage."

"And the other half?"

"You still don't see? Or what you've done to us? You don't think the children suffered from that?"

"Well they never see me now — does that make it any better?"

"It does," she said. "They have no expectations."

"But they belong to me — I don't care what the court says!"

Luana trembled with anger. "I raised them, and I decide who they belong to, don't you understand? I decide what they need — and you've proven you are not what they need!"

"Luana, I have changed!"

"Only your feelings have changed!" She calmed again and walked to the door, turned, and folded her arms. "You honestly believe that the man who always has to sail the seven seas in you is gone?"

Porter just stared at her.

"If it's one thing I learned," she continued, "it's what makes up your soul. Domestic you're not. A farmer you're not. My husband, you're not. You realize what you've lost, and you want to be different, but that doesn't work for us because you are the same man."

"And what's wrong with that?"

"I suppose nothing by itself. But my family are farmers. And my children will be. We're two different sorts, and we cannot live together."

"That's a choice you're making," he said, "but it's not based on me being right or wrong. There's nothing wrong with me being something in my heart other than a farmer."

"I agree with you completely," she said. "So go back to your causes and your excitement and your danger."

He studied the floor. "You don't understand anything about me . . . What I want most is a peaceful life — just not as a farmer."

"It's more than that — you're an adventurer. Maybe not a danger-seeker. Maybe I was wrong. But you are an adventurer, and you ever will be. The river life is a perfect example of that."

"That doesn't make me unfit."

"Not unfit as a person, you're right," she said. "Only unfit for me. So can't we just leave it at that?"

His face flustered with frustration.

"If you really want to know, Porter . . . I simply don't even care anymore. Doesn't that tell you anything?"

Porter gazed up from the floor to her penetrating eyes.

"And if you come to talk like this again," she added, "or for any other purpose than to visit the children, I'm having your visiting time with Emily cut in half. Is that clear enough?"

Porter gazed down again, too hurt to even look at her, and he walked out the door.

Emily walked in, overhearing from a back room. "Mama, I want to go with him."

Luana replied, "No, Emily. You can see him tomorrow."
Emily ran outside to him.

Porter stopped and turned to Emily, "It's safe here — I got some dangerous business to take care of. I'll come for you in a few days."

"Why not tomorrow?" persisted Emily, hugging him.

"Maybe. But there's bad things happening in the city," he said. "By bad people that can hurt us. I need to protect our city, and it's not safe for you to be with me sometimes. Alright?"

She nodded, looking up at him with eyes wide, feeling for him as her true father now more than ever.

"Bye, bye, honey," he said, kissing her forehead and striding away to his horse.

She smiled, knowing as always he would be back for her. She loved him more than she could put into words.

CHAPTER 30

Porter listened to the heated debate. A dozen city council-men argued over what they should do with the *Nauvoo Expositor*. It was June 10, 1844.

"Destroy it!" said one. "New York police destroy scurrilous presses every year, and Article B of the Illinois Constitution allows us to eliminate slanderous presses."

"But what about freedom of the press?" said another.

"Freedom of the press does not cover slanderous rags!"

One of their council members, Benjamin Warrington, who was not of their faith, argued, "I consider this all rather harsh."

"The trouble is," pointed out another, "what if people outside our city believe this? They'll bring mobs against us, just like in Missouri!"

"Then I propose an alternative," countered Warrington. "I propose we merely fine the editors $3,000 for every libel."

"The trouble with that," said Hyrum, "is these men don't have money for fines. But even if they did, would they quit publishing?"

"Also," said Joseph, "we have another problem. If we sued them for libel we'd have to take them to court at Carthage. We'll get nowhere there."

"But gentlemen," said another, "we're forgetting something. What will the governor think if we actually destroy the press?"

They all thought for a moment in silence. Another finally broke the silence, "He supports the law, doesn't he?"

Spoke another, "The law is clearly on our side."

Porter said nothing, but suspected they had no other alternative. Yet, he knew if they did destroy it, they would be opening the flood gates.

The city council took a vote, and the majority decided to eliminate the press. It formally issued an order to Joseph, as mayor, to "Destroy the establishment as a nuisance."

Joseph turned to the city marshal and ordered him to eliminate it without delay. A city posse would have it destroyed, and Porter was assigned to go with them.

Porter did not look forward to it. Before sunset he and nine others in uniform marched down Mulholland Street to the site of the press. Their leader, Marshal Greene, knocked at the door.

Francis Higbee answered it, saw them, and immediately shut it. Greene shoved the door with his shoulder and it flew opened.

Porter and the others entered, tied a knot around the press and pulled it outside. In the street they also gathered the type, fixtures, and printed papers, and set fire to them. Meanwhile

Marshal Greene handed Higbee a city council order. Higbee began screaming and swearing.

The posse, under orders, remained calm, even courteous to Higbee.

"Porter, you tell Smith this city is dead!" shouted Higbee as the posse left the office. "I will personally bury it!"

Porter nodded to him and left. Although he had opposed the action in his heart, he had enjoyed every second.

CHAPTER 31

Warsaw, Illinois had 500 inhabitants. It was 15½ miles south of Nauvoo and 14½ miles southwest of Carthage, forming a triangle in frontier Illinois. It was also the home of Thomas Sharp's *Warsaw Signal* newspaper. Sharp was the man Porter had seen at the Hamilton House shortly after his return from Liberty Jail before someone had sent a vigilante group chasing him in the woods.

Sharp now sat at the editor's desk of the *Signal,* listening. He was an affable man who bore himself without a trace of self-consciousness. And today he was entertained by the story of Chauncey and Francis Higbee, Augustin Spencer, and William and Wilson Law, who sat across his desk.

To Sharp they seemed so serious about their account and yet so near-sighted that it struck within him an amusing chord.

"We got the first issue of the *Nauvoo Expositor* published and right away the city council destroyed it," complained Chauncey Higbee. "Joseph is afraid the non-Mormon populace will be stirred into a frenzy," he added. "And that's why they destroyed the press. But we can publish anything we please. So we took it to court in Nauvoo. There, William Law officially brought complaints against city officials, including Joseph, for destroying the *Expositor.* We also claimed Joseph's people started a riot. However the Nauvoo court claimed there was no riot, and it decided our suit was malicious and even made us pay the court costs!"

"Who did you sue?" said Sharp.

"All the city councilmen and Joseph Smith."

Sharp knew a hot story when he saw one, and he knew this time he was going to exploit the daylights out of it. He did not particularly dislike the Mormons' viewpoint against slavery, but their other doctrines annoyed him, and he felt he possessed a remarkable, if not downright enviable, talent for stirring controversy whenever he had the opportunity. He especially felt Joseph possessed far too much power, and that his self-ordained mission was to protect his readers. Primarily, he now saw an opportunity to effectually double his circulation. He knew thousands of potential readers — and advertisers — in and around three counties were eyeing the fertile Mormon stronghold that Smith had built up. And that, given his own life-long position at the bottom wrung of the family financial ladder, was an incentive he could not easily let pass him by. His wife was a kindly woman, his two children obedient and thrifty. He had asked them to sacrifice long enough. He loved his wife, and he had stewed silently at the family gatherings when she would stare wide-eyed at his brothers' fine apparel and stately horses. Sharp knew she was silently envious of their wives, but through seven years of marriage she had said nothing. She was a woman of such depth, Sharp realized, that her love for him was not conditional on his financial success. Nevertheless, he was determined that one day she would be proud of him. His autumn eyebrows were a shade lighter than his bushy, dark red sideburns, and they both starkly highlighted his intense, blue eyes. He reflected on the story of the several men before him.

"I want you gentlemen to assist me," he said. "After I print this story, I want you to take a copy to every newspaper in the state, and I want in writing from every editor that my paper gets the by-line. Is that clear?"

The conspirators waited in a Warsaw tavern downstreet while Thomas Sharp polished the article from his interview notes. He read aloud his favorite and final paragraph just before he would set it to type for today's issue of the *Warsaw Signal:*

"We must put an immediate stop to the career of the mad prophet and his demonic coadjutors. We must not only defend ourselves from this danger, but we must carry the war into the enemy's camp. Thos S. Sharp, editor." (Author's note: This was the actual text.)

Sharp felt a tingle he hadn't felt in years. He had attempted to build his paper for so many years on so many schemes, and had tried so many various promotions with such negligible results, that something this time told him deep down this might be his last opportunity to really cash in on something big. And it was especially satisfying, knowing his own intense distaste for the Mormon power structure.

CHAPTER 32

Porter and Joseph were now returning from a non-Mormon court appearance outside Hancock County. There, they had just been exonerated from shutting down the *Expositor* newspaper, as the court had found them operating within Illinois state law. Joseph had agreed to the court because, since it was out of the area, he figured more objectivity might exist. But, upon returning, he feared Nauvoo could be attacked any hour — ironically because of the court declaring him and the city council innocent.

Tonight while riding to Nauvoo they passed a village where citizens were meeting under a torchlight and listening to a speaker reading aloud Sharp's article calling for arms to be raised against Nauvoo. The people cheered. Porter and Joseph traveled beside the road under the cover of trees, their faces dappled by moonlight, and they said not a word, both thinking what the other was thinking — and seeing the same old cycle of violence re-forming.

Added to Porter's frustrations was his inability to shake from his mind Luana' simple beauty, exemplified by wrinkles of character and years of trial on her face, with rugged, rough hands from honest toil, plus her wide-eyed expression of vulnerability that always had charmed him. She could not be matched by any other woman, he feared. Not ever.

Under the moonlight as they re-entered Nauvoo, Porter beheld Pisces brightly lighting the firmament. The city was quiet. Without a word to his riding companion, he turned his horse away. He had to check on his family's dwelling, hoping to find it safe, concerned more than ever about his children during these hours of increasing uncertainty.

He arrived at Luana's once again and expressed his concerns of the family's safety to Alpheas Cutler. Luana of course would not see him. Cutler made no comment, but escorted him to the back of their property to visit the children. He did not care for Porter's innuendo that he could not protect the family, and thus rejected Porter's offer of assistance to that end.

Porter held up each one, then played tag with them. A breeze rustled the trees and the moonlight's orange light cast a glow on his children that made them particularly angelic. Especially Emily, who presently came out the back door and hugged him. She animatedly told him of her day. Then she showed him a painting she had started. It was leaning against the cabin, drying, and was a remarkable oil rendition of the Nauvoo Temple at dawn. In reality the temple was far from completed, but in the painting it stood fully constructed in all its majesty. Porter was in the painting standing beside Emily.

Porter remarked on its realism. Soon Luana emerged from the house to greet him. Unexpected by her visit, he gazed at her, wanting to reveal his deepest feelings, but merely thanked her for the chance to visit with the kids, and left. Luana felt relieved he did not press any other subjects, and that he had evidently given up on her. Cutler then walked up to her. She turned to him and blew out a silent sigh. She was somewhat disconcerted however when Alpheas suddenly blurted out loudly enough for Porter to hear all the way around the cabin:

"I hoped those idiots who clubbed the *Expositor* get the justice they deserve."

Porter stopped and walked back to them. "Did you say something to me?"

Luana saw a fight coming and blushed with fear for Alpheas.

"Every law-abiding citizen must be concerned," said Alpheas. "Don't you think?"

Porter stopped right in front of Cutler.

"'You support their views?" said Porter.

"I see no reason why they shouldn't print their views. Haven't you heard of freedom of the press?"

"You didn't answer my question."

"I'm not certain how many of their views I agree with, but they have the right to their viewpoints, don't you think?"

"I think you're having problems following Joseph," said Porter, who turned to walk away.

Cutler got louder, "Ask Joseph himself — does he think he's above the law? He thinks he can destroy any newspaper he doesn't agree with?"

Porter merely shook his head, still walking away.

"You're just going to turn your back on questions that hurt? Is that how high and mighty you are now, Porter?"

Cutler ran up to him and grabbed Porter's shirt, turning him around to face him. Luana tried to intervene, but Cutler pushed her out of the way. He then shoved Porter, "Answer me!"

Porter shoved him back and shouted, "Don't you dare touch that woman like that again!"

"Porter, stay out of it!" shouted Luana. "Just answer me!" said Cutler.

Porter stood directly in front of his eyes. "Nobody's high and mighty around here — but the city council decided on the fate of that press — I was there and I heard 'em. Not Joseph. And they've got the law on their side. But I fear some folks in this city are too ignorant to check that out, Cutler. If I hear any more talk in front of my kids like that — or they tell me about it — you're going to wish you'd never met me." He then shoved Cutler again — harder — and Cutler toppled down into the mud, swearing.

Porter walked away, glanced back, and beheld his entire family gawking at him. He was embarrassed for his actions. He lowered his head and kept walking. But Emily was beaming. Porter mumbled to them all:

"I'm sorry."

He mounted his roan and rode off, mumbling to himself, "What a sorry mess."

———————

Before he had ridden three blocks, he passed the Higbee home and spotted Chauncey Higbee exiting. Porter moved his eyes to the road that led to Joseph's home and the peace he would find there but, at the same moment, his curiosity ached over Higbee's plans.

Higbee, without seeing him, mounted and rode the opposite direction.

Porter glanced down Joseph's road again, then, gazing back at Higbee, sighed and decided to follow the man.

CHAPTER 33

In Carthage, Higbee dismounted. Porter was still following him, and observed him entering the Hamilton House. Inside, he spotted Higbee across the tavern — sitting with several of the conspirators.

Porter advanced carefully through the crowded room in order to not be seen, his long hair tucked under a high collar and his hat pulled low. He seated himself two tables away yet within ear-shot of a loud Robert Foster, whose voice boomed from a bit much whiskey.

Porter did not catch all the details, but enough to send a shiver across his neck: He heard pieces of plans about a lynch mob — it would attack from the river shore and hit Joseph's home first. Then the mobbers would take Joseph prisoner before the Nauvoo Legion could be alerted, and hang him in Carthage. Next, they would march on Joseph's newspaper, the *Nauvoo Neighbor,* and burn it before morning.

Stunned at the news, Porter eased his way through the standing, talking bodies, and hurried out the doorway.

That night, Porter warned Joseph of the impending attack. Joseph immediately ordered Hyrum to gather the Nauvoo Legion to defend the city.

Porter watched Hyrum leave the room, and regarded his efficiency as he ordered other associates to prepare the city for war. Porter reflected that, since childhood, Hyrum was the one Joseph could most trust.

If ever a loyalty existed between two men, Porter thought, it existed between Hyrum and Joseph Smith. They had never spoken harshly to one another in all the years he had known them, and their mutual respect seemed intransigent. Nor had Hyrum seemed to mind his brother's tendency to order him about when Joseph was excited, and today was no exception. By contrast, Porter noted, Rigdon, the Laws and others generally flinched at Joseph's commands. Other, less-ranking souls in the kingdom never questioned Joseph, just those very competent, very charismatic, articulate fellows Joseph surrounded himself with who could get things accomplished better than others could but whom Porter suspected as being too proud for their own good and, as events were bearing out, were actually vying for leadership — complete leadership — with Joseph out of the way. Throughout it all, friends observed that the Smith brothers had a bond that was unbreakable, a bond which Porter appreciated as well. He was also proud that both brothers accepted him as a brother, albeit a younger one whose counsels were not always regarded as highly as he would like;

nevertheless, he was aware of the roles men retain since childhood, and he was grateful to just be a part of the brotherhood.

Porter finished watching Hyrum sketch out battle plans to defend the city, then left the Mansion House. As he walked away, he decided to further fight his feelings of fear for his family and join the Nauvoo Legion's stand-off against the on-coming lynch mob.

The woods surrounding Nauvoo provided natural cover for the several hundred Nauvoo Legionnaires guarding the city that night.

Under the moonlight, Porter, dressed in uniform, seemed out-of-form as his long hair swirled in the breeze. He rode the new horse given him by Joseph, and took position with the brigade southeast of the city. His excitement for an impending confrontation tempered the painful thoughts of his family, yet he simultaneously worried about their welfare in case the mob were not stopped.

Not stopped.

The horror consumed his mind for a moment. If anyone had to be most pivital in stopping the mob, he knew it was he. His eyes darted about the woods.

He arose.

He strode to his commanding officer and requested an assignment as forward guard.

"Are you insane?" said his commander.

"Maybe."

Porter was now 200 yards in front of the infantry, and in tall grass he waited. He knew Joseph's blessing was in effect and that no one else should risk his life needlessly. He was surprised at his own faith. Secretly, he also wondered if he did not harbor a death wish.

The stars shone brightly when, through the woods, he caught sight of the lynch mob moving near the river.

He took out his pistol and cocked it. He realized he could not retreat in time to sound a warning to his men, or the mob would be upon him. Although Joseph's blessing was one of protection from bullet and blade, he knew he could not tempt heaven and blatantly put himself in harm's way. After all, there was nothing said about not being clubbed to death! So he decided to merely stay put and study his enemy. He saw in their faces the same murder-lust and prejudice he had seen in Missouri when his people had been attacked. Then he realized what he really now desired: an all-out battle. He was surprised to discover his own heart beating decidedly harder at the thought. He wished to see his own army's rifles cut these cowards to shreds. He wanted nothing less than a slaughter. He desired to take out on them all he had lived through at Independence and Liberty jails. He could tell from their sounds that half of them were soused. The others were drinking as they walked. The Nauvoo Legion could have a field day.

His lower lip quivered. He could launch the massacre himself by shooting their leader 50 yards ahead — Frank Worrell

— then take off running back to his lines, leading the frenzied mob into a trap.

From that thought, however, he realized the consequences: An army combined from several states could march on Nauvoo within days, and Joseph's peace strategy would be entirely thwarted. Then, again, he could show the mobs what they're really made of and perhaps win some respect — and some second thoughts — about presenting his people future problems.

The lynch mob came closer, and Porter beheld 300 men. Then, once again, he arose.

The mob spotted him and stopped. He heard mutterings, but Frank Worrell held them at bay. Worrell finally called out.

"Soldier, 'you alone?'"

"Come forward and find out," said Porter.

CHAPTER 34

Frank Worrell's signature calling was that of an outstanding Carthage citizen. He was tall, charming, and considered a lady's man. At 47, he owned the largest hardware shop in the county.

Frank did not know Porter by identity but had heard from Chauncey Higbee about the long hair. He gazed over his men, many of whom were now yelling to "attack the woman in uniform."

Another of Worrell's vigilantes called out, "What have we got to lose?"

"Just step forward," shouted Porter, "and learn the answer to that question, too."

Suddenly 600 rifle bolts shattered the air in unison. Rifles were cocked and ready to fire. It was the Nauvoo Legion. They had heard the commotion and advanced to Porter's position without his cognizance.

From the sudden, terrifying clash of metal, Worrell's eyes went wide, and he shouted to his men, "Retreat!"

"Hold fire!" a legionnaire officer yelled.

Porter watched as the mob threw themselves into a panic and ran in a frenzy across the woods and disappeared. Porter smiled as he watched them run. Some were stumbling from too much drink, others were cursing the vines and stumps over which they were tripping. Porter then heard, inexplicably — and perhaps driven from the sudden release of tension — his 600 legionnaires suddenly burst out chuckling.

Frank Worrell heard the derisive laughter and took it as a personal challenge. He grimaced and decided he would see Porter in his grave someday — immediately after first taking care of Joseph Smith. And then he'd see who'd laugh the *most* triumphantly.

At the Mansion House, Porter reported the episode to Joseph, who was busy preparing a speech to his legionnaires. He listened carefully, then blew out a sigh.

"Porter, I want you to be on the look-out during my speech tonight. Watch among the civilians if you will."

"For who?"

"Who else?"

"The conspirators."

Approximately one in six members of the community were members of the 2,000-strong Nauvoo Legion, which was even larger than the state militia. Joseph knew they could find themselves in a precarious position unless they were well-trained, and thus they were. He also knew the press was still having a field-day, and that Thomas Sharp was leading the way. Other newspapers in surrounding counties were picking up his stories, as Sharp had planned, and printing them as substantiated truth, and there was even talk that local militia might form to attack the city.

Joseph asked Porter to attend a meeting that was about to start. First, however, Porter returned to his bedroom to think about what else he could do for his family. He had no answers. His head clear, he went downstairs to the conference. John Taylor and Hyrum Smith were discussing with Joseph how they could deal with the bad press. He entered the southwest parlor and chose instinctively a high-backed Jacobean chair that had somewhat the air of a throne.

Visiting observers to the Mansion House agreed the furniture gave one a feeling of solidity. Partly because of that, Porter enjoyed visiting Joseph's home whenever occasion would permit. Emma, of course, would just as soon see him up in his room with his dog. Ugly, incidentally, had been spending his days lazily lounging along the Mississippi River. Emma had the unfortunate task of feeding it whenever Porter was gone for the day, and at this he was ever amused. If Porter were to be gone for more than a day, he'd take the animal to his mother, Sarah, to care for it.

Emma soon entered the parlor, and with her usual, royal composure presented the gentlemen with tea.

She glared at Porter, not particularly pleased that he always chose her favorite chair, especially in his usually scruffy condition. "At least he bathes often," she would confide privately to Joseph, searching for something positive, although for some reason she did not particularly care for the man nor his ugly dog.

Porter meanwhile cast a gaze on her, thinking she was very beautiful, but not in any way he would want a woman — more as a painting to admire yet for which to be grateful it did not hang on his own wall.

That night, Joseph stood in uniform atop the Mansion House. He practically glowed with his characteristic aura that mesmerized his people, and he boomed his voice to two thousand volunteer soldiers.

Porter left the front ranks to watch from a side angle for enemy spies in their midst. He thought he spotted Francis Higbee at the back of a crowd of civilians. As he squinted his eyes, he was certain it was indeed Higbee. Then the suspicion overcame him that Higbee just very likely might be carrying a weapon . . .

CHAPTER 35

Higbee made his way through the crowd as Joseph spoke with conviction:

"I call God, angels and all men to witness that we are innocent of the charges heralded forth through the public prints against us by our enemies; and while they assemble together in unlawful mobs to take away our rights and destroy our lives, they think to shield themselves under the refuge of lies which they have fabricated.

"Will you all stand by me to the death, and sustain at the peril of your lives the laws of our country and the liberties and privileges which our fathers have transmitted unto us, sealed with their sacred blood?"

The soldiers responded with a thunderous, "Aye!"

Joseph drew his sword to the sky, "I call God and angels to witness that I have unsheathed my sword with a firm and unalterable determination that this people shall have their legal rights, and be protected from mob violence, or my blood shall be spilt upon the ground like water and my body consigned to the silent tomb." (Author's note: This was the actual text of his speech.)

As Joseph closed his remarks, Porter closed in on the last spot where he had seen Higbee. As he arrived there, Higbee was gone.

He then spotted Higbee's horse galloping downroad, disappearing into the night.

At the Warsaw Signal, a brick building east of the Warsaw Hotel on Main Street 15½ miles south, Thomas Sharp sat at his desk to proofread. He was proud that from years of hard toil in the pressroom his own hands were worn, warty, gnarly and knobby. His face was sallow and drawn, suffering from little sleep over his all-out circulation enhancement campaign. Despite the exhaustion, his success was a source of substantial pride to him. He glanced up and noticed Augustine Spencer and Wilson Law entering with drawn faces.

Thomas Sharp cleared his throat. "Frank Worrell just told me of the lynch mob and their attack on Nauvoo. You gentlemen are disappointing me," he said, smiling. He actually wanted a protracted conflict because newspaper sales were booming, and the longer his little war continued, the better the sales, he mused.

Law picked up a glass paperweight from Sharp's desk.

Sharp was concerned. It was a family heirloom. But he said nothing.

Law tossed the glass sphere into the air and caught it, then heaved it to Sharp, who caught it and set it down with a sigh. Sharp boomed, "What we need is something to galvanize the community against Joseph. I'm sorry, did I say community? I mean communities — every community in three counties — even more."

He realized if he could set up a cost-effective circulation in such a broad area, he would be taking major steps at achieving his profit objectives. "And if they were all moved to action simultaneously," he continued, "Smith's force would pale by comparison."

"So what's our plan?" said Spencer, now picking up the paperweight to his eye and examining it closely.

"The appropriate article about the appropriate incident," said Sharp, now standing, beaming, feeling actually exhilarated. "Give me that thing, would you?" He snatched the glass object from Spencer's grasp. He fumbled it a second and it crashed to the ground, splintering into a thousand pieces.

Sharp swore, and knelt to brush it into a dustpan.

Francis Higbee then entered, animated, and told Sharp of Joseph's fiery speech.

"It sounds like a full-scale war," summarized Higbee.

As Sharp reflected on the effect that Joseph's speech would have on even greater circulation and advertising revenue he picked up one final glass piece, and cut himself. He cursed again, and blood dripped onto the floor. "I think," said Sharp, "that Joseph and his people are going to learn what a full-scale war really looks like."

CHAPTER 36

Under a grey sky there was not a breath of wind. Riding horseback, Porter was lost in thought. He wondered if he were indeed what Luana thought — an incurable adventurer. He took his ride deeper into the country, craving solitude. After an hour he decided to water his horse. He dismounted at a stream and sat with his back propped against an oak. His mind searched the sky as he recalled his earlier years with Luana.

Two hours later he was again riding, the sun splashing rays through trees onto him. A faint fog rolled in. He could smell the warm scent of the soil as the red sun settled behind the mist. Then the fog lifted on one side of him only.

He rode through twilight wondering what he should do. He realized that Joseph, whom he would like to confide in, was still consumed by affairs of the state and the state of affairs. He realized he had never felt such loneliness, not even in jail, because there at least he had hope. Now, for the first time in his life, he felt absolute hopelessness. He fought the depression descending on him. No other woman could even begin to attract him, he felt; he rarely even met single women; when he did they always bored him. As he thought of Cutler's affections to Luana, it cut him in half. He pondered his future, realizing that even their entire civilization they'd built from swamps into Illinois' greatest city could be destined to ruin. He considered the possibility of leaving Nauvoo, defecting from his people and protecting himself from probable imprisonment. He could be a bartender in New Orleans, he mused. Perhaps he could escape to a new life — California — or even Europe.

An early star twinkled palely close to the horizon. His concerns scorched his mind. He simply did not know what to do, or where to go.

Ahead was a campfire. Perhaps human company is all he needed. He perceived two hundred yards ahead six or eight men engaged in an activity. He looked forward to sitting at the fire, listening to the simple chatter of Carthage rurals. Not all were prejudiced and perhaps these were more friendly than most. His curiosity was struck by what they were doing at the fire. He dismounted, tied his horse and sauntered forward, still unobserved. He hesitated behind thick bushes and could barely discern the men, yet he could hear them clearly.

Six men had another surrounded whom they questioned vigorously. Leading them was none other than Frank Worrell.

"Ain't interested," said the man being questioned. He was an older fellow, medium but frail, and had long, bushy sideburns and no hair on top. Porter recognized him as Alexander Tillman, owner of a merchandizing distributorship which sold to all western Illinois general stores.

"Look, maybe I ain't clear," said Worrell. "You don't have a choice."

"And maybe I ain't clear — I ain't interested."

"Well, I've seen how the judges interpret the law," Worrell added.

"But the Mormons will put up a fight — they won't just deliver Smith over to you."

"Then you can fight for one side or the other, or share the same fate as them," said Worrell.

"Yeah, we'll see," said Tillman. But if you touch my property, I'm coming after you."

"Who's touching your property? Just sign this contract, and Joseph's people can buy from somebody else."

"Nobody else has the merchandise I've got. They need my goods. They'll be hurt without it. I'll be hurt without the sales."

Worrell fumed. He was not used to being crossed. He had never considered himself a particularly violent man, but for the sake of what he believed in nothing could get in his way, and he was almost daily surprising himself with the extent to which he could go to accomplish what simply needed to be accomplished. He grabbed Tillman and shoved him towards the fire.

Porter moved instinctively forward, not certain what he would do, particularly since he was unarmed, but he was certain of one thing: He was not going to leave old Alex Tillman stranded to be veritably burned at the stake . . .

CHAPTER 37

$\mathbf{F}$rank Worrell's five men watched as Worrell lowered Tillman to the fire, the flames within a foot of his back. Tillman began to wince from the pain . . .

"Just sign the contract, "said Worrell. "And we'll all have our fires quenched."

Tillman was a stubborn goat. He would rather sizzle than sign anything against his will. And he was determined to not give Worrell the satisfaction of hearing him scream. Five seconds later he was inches from the flames and the heat began scorching him. His face contorted as he felt the pain shooting through his back.

Suddenly, a body came belting out of the forest and it lunged into Worrell's back. Tillman sprawled to the side and Worrell plunged forward off balance . . . directly into the flames. He screamed and scrambled to his feet, his coat ablaze.

Porter grabbed Worrell's pistol and pointed it at the other five.

"You better help your buddy," said Porter. "Or he's gonna roast himself."

But the five men merely stood there in shock while Worrell shouted, still in flames, "Put it out, you idiots!"

Porter glanced them over and gave them a command. "He's right. Roll him on the ground, idiots."

One of Worrell's men grabbed Worrell's left arm and flung him to the ground. Two others rolled him in the dirt, extinguishing the fire on his coat. "I can't breathe, you mud-suckin' fools. Get off!"

Porter ordered Tillman to mount his horse, then tossed cold canteen water on his back. Porter snatched the contract from the ground, stepped up to the fire, and dropped the paper into the flames. "I don't think you'll be needing this," he said to Worrell. As the men watched the burning paper, one poured cold water on Worrell's back. Porter continued, "I reckon you oughta leave Tillman's property alone or you're gonna see flames on somebody's property."

When he disappeared into the woods, Worrell leered at him.

"Yeah, we'll see whose property sees flames."

Joseph swatted a newspaper against the table, frustrated at Porter's humiliating Frank Worrell.

"What did you expect me to do, let Tillman fry?" said Porter.

"I think you know what I mean about riling up Worrell."

"What's happened since I was gone?" said Porter.

"I'm getting reports of armed horsemen from across the countryside gathering at Carthage."

"So what do we do now?" said Porter.

Almon Babbitt entered, holding a copy of the *Warsaw Signal.* Babbitt was a friend of Joseph's and a Mormon attorney; he was a recent convert who sought more than anything the adulation he felt due him from Joseph. He considered Joseph as bright as himself, perhaps the only man in fact he had ever met with such cerebral heft. Babbitt was an extroverted, short, stocky man, three inches shorter than Porter, and he possessed a wide fleshy nose with large nostrils. People liked him for his ebullient spirit and gregariousness. He was extremely competent and had a mind, some said, sharper than a bear trap.

But when Porter saw him, the hair on the back of his head arose. It was Babbitt whom Luana had retained as her attorney in filing divorce papers and, Porter figured, who had nailed into her mind the desertion of his kids and courting the wife of Amos Davis as issues, the latter of which was equally preposterous to Porter but which a suspicious mind like Luana's had been quick to consider and, even if she knew were not true, would be a justifiable reason in any judge's eyes to grant the divorce she so desperately desired. Babbitt had seen the Davis wife issue as a sure-fire legal tactic, even though he had heard a few rumors and figured they were in fact only rumors. Porter had actually engaged himself in a few conversations with the lady upon seeing her in stores about town, finding her a sympathetic listener and eventually a rather charming, flirtatious soul who seemed to be developing a crush on him, so he had cut off the friendship when his conscience was pricked. Later, Luana brought to his attention the rumors circulating about, and she seemed to brush them off as mere gossip — this was all just prior to his Philadelphia journey. Upon his return from jail, Porter had run across Davis' wife only once and, on that occasion, had tipped his hat politely but had not stopped to talk, so he was therefore surprised when he was told the divorce papers had included "other women" as an issue. He had been equally frustrated with Luana and her attorney for such court manipulations, and knew deep down, the more he thought about it, that it was more legal strategm than something Luana truly believed. Thus, he was not too pleased with Babitt, who now stood beside Joseph's desk.

"Porter," said Joseph, "you remember Almon Babbitt."

Porter forced a smile.

"Let by-gones be by-gones, old friend," said Babbitt. "I'd have represented you just as thoroughly."

"I'd only want thoroughness that includes truth," said Porter with a grimace.

"Sore losers?" smiled Babbitt, looking up at the taller Rockwell as if tempting him for a fight.

"You could see how sore a loser can get," answered Rockwell, slightly clenching his fists.

"That's enough, boys," said Joseph. "Porter, go get a breath of fresh air, please. I'll be out soon."

Porter blew out a long silent sigh. "I'm all right." He then sat and stared at the two men, realizing he needed to let go of blaming Luana's hired gun. Babbitt certainly had no fight with him, and Babbitt now actually winked at him, then turned to Joseph.

"Did you see the article?" said Babbitt.

Joseph answered by moving his eyes to a newspaper on the table.

"So what do you think?" continued Joseph's new friend.

"There's only one thing I can do at this point," said Joseph. "I've got to put the entire city under martial law."

Babbitt was frantic. "You're not serious. The press will have a field day."

"They already have," said Joseph. "I have no alternative."

Porter left the Mansion House even more depressed. He was convinced the persecutions were stepping up with even greater acceleration than they had in Missouri. The whole city would be coming down like a house of cards.

Beside a stream, Porter stared at his reflection. Although the animal-like image from his deprivation in jail no longer appeared, his new look revealed a deep, inner burning. Yet the pain he felt — mainly over his children — was enhanced by an impending, developing war he could smell in the air.

He had come to the woods to think once again, but now felt a gnawing curiosity beckoning him back to the Mansion House. He mounted his roan, trotted through the woods, and found himself cantering down a peaceful country lane. A brisk, warm breeze filled his nostrils with rich woodland odors.

Birds chirped cheerily.

The air cooled quickly. A late afternoon thunder cloud rolled in from the East.

He decided to pick up his horse's gait.

Clouds darkened. Before he could reach Nauvoo, rain began pouring. Soon he heard thunder. On adjacent roads across the country he heard the roar of hooves — horsehooves — hundreds of horsehooves. He glanced to both sides of the road and realized in a flash that the hordes of horsemen were only rods away — on parallel roads that converged onto his, not more than fifty yards distant.

He rode off the main road into the cover of woods. He spotted a cabin being plundered. The family was fleeing. Porter had with him less ammunition than usual and determined it best not to confront the small army. He rode deeper into the forest.

Another farm was being attacked: Horsemen tied ropes to the roof and pulled it off. As the rain poured into the roofless cabin, the family fled.

Porter raced toward the city. He came across other families on the road. In anger he broke into a gallop, the mud flinging high.

Fully drenched from the rain, he arrived at the Mansion House and rushed inside.

CHAPTER 38

Joseph Smith stood at a window in his study, staring at the storm.

"I reckon," said Porter, "you've heard."

Joseph ignored him, lost in thought.

Hyrum was seated across the room holding a letter, and read it to Porter.

It was from Governor Ford, now in nearby Carthage. Ford had come to investigate the *Expositor* affair first-hand. The letter demanded Joseph to send representatives to tell his side of the story.

"Well I'm glad he wants at least that," said Porter.

"You don't understand," argued Hyrum. "All it means is the conspirators have reached the governor with their side of the story first. No telling how many days they've been filling him with lies."

"At least we have a chance to tell our side," said Porter.

"I'm afraid it's useless," said Hyrum. "The governor's aides have made no bones about their animosity towards us. And with the conspirators' affidavits as fuel, I'm certain by now his aides have completely turned him against us."

"There's still some kind of chance," said Porter.

"What chance?" said Hyrum. "Ford's a consummate politician. He sees what Sharp has done with public opinion, and whether he agrees with it or not I doubt is even the issue at this point. We haven't a chance in Hades."

"There's even a chance in Hades," said Joseph. He turned to Hyrum and asked him to send a delegation to Carthage, led by Porter to protect them.

Almon Babbitt strode briskly in the door, having overheard his last sentence. "Forget the delegation — I just came from Carthage." They all regarded him curiously.

"Rabble are threatening death on sight to anyone who even sets foot in the city," continued Babbitt.

Porter stood. "I'll get through."

"Don't send anyone," demanded Babbitt.

Porter glowered at him.

Joseph continued, "I'm sorry, Almon, but I do have to send a delegation to the governor to explain our side of the story."

"Then don't send Rockwell," said Babbitt, still glaring at Porter. "The press has made him their favorite target. If he represents us they'll play it to the hilt."

"So?" said Porter.

"We'll have war."

"What do you think we have now?" said Porter.

Joseph finally turned to John Taylor, well-known for his diplomacy among non-Mormons. "John, you're our man."

With his peaceful yet fearless demeanor John Taylor successfully made it past the mobs to the governor's temporary office in Carthage. There, Taylor presented Joseph's side of the *Expositor* issue. He explained to Governor Ford that a non-Mormon magistrate named Wells had legally exonerated Joseph outside of Hancock County on the destruction of the *Expositor.*

The next night John Taylor returned up Carthage Road, turned onto Partridge, then Water Street, and dismounted at the Mansion House. Joseph, Porter, Hyrum and others waited to hear his report. All looked on him anxiously. Taylor cleared his throat and finally spoke:

"Governor Ford has decided to try you and Hyrum in court — along with 13 others."

Joseph was stunned.

"What the devil for!" shouted Porter. "A dozen more of our homes were unroofed last night!"

Taylor continued, "He promised you safety, Joseph, if you turn yourself over to county authorities."

A gloom fell over the men. They knew how dangerous Carthage was and doubted Ford's ability to stop stray gun shots. Joseph walked to the window and stared outside. After a moment he turned, his face gleaming from the kerosene light. "We could try to resist the militia with our troops, and there would

RICHARD LLOYD DEWEY

be a bloodbath, but I see another way. The Spirit of the Lord has just revealed to me the only opportunity to escape without loss of life . . . and it is now. It is time for us to move."

They stared at him incredulously. Porter suddenly felt a surge of hope.

"Where?" said Hyrum.

"To the Great Basin of the Rocky Mountains. I have seen it in vision. But it all now depends on just one thing — our people's willingness to pick up and move on, as they've done before. But this time, they can go without being forced to leave their homes. This time it's a choice."

The men gazed at him curiously.

CHAPTER 39

Luana opened her door. Porter stood there, eyes wide and panicked. He had galloped to her home from the Mansion House.

"Get the kids ready, and tell Alpheas to pack your valuables," he said.

"What're you talking about?"

"I found an old row boat. I'm taking Joseph, Hyrum and Willard across the river, then I'm coming for you."

"Porter, I thought you accepted it's over between us. And I did tell you what I'd do if you kept showing up here without warning."

"You didn't mind when I got Emily every night."

"We knew you were coming then, but I'd never come to the door to greet you, if you'll remember. You're only welcome here without warning to put out a fire or something, am I clear?"

"There is a fire, and that's what I'm saving you from. You're moving."

"You think I'd just pack up everything and move?"

"Of course."

"We're not crazy, Porter. We're not moving again! It took years finally finding a place to call home and building it up. Look at that garden — and those fences — and this home! The children are settled — they have friends, a place we all love, and we're not leaving it just because of some hair-brained scheme of yours!"

"Luana, Joseph has spoken! We can save his life if we move on!"

"To where!"

"The Rocky Mountains!"

"You are crazy!"

"It'll only take hours to get your most important stuff together, and some food, and I'll be back before dawn and we can make our getaway. Alpheas can help. I'm not trying to take his place."

"You haven't heard me, have you? Don't you think I lived that way long enough — if you call moving living."

"Then at least get the kids ready!"

"Get off my property."

"You're leaving them here to get mobbed?"

"If you don't want the city mobbed, you get Joseph to do what it takes so we aren't mobbed. It's up to him! Is that clear?"

"Joseph is not surrendering."

"If he breaks the law and destroys someone's press, he should . . . "

Porter interrupted, "He did not break the law, and he ain't surrendering!"

"Then that's his mistake!"

"It's your mistake to hang on to useless property! This land is nothing without Joseph! And neither is this city!"

Luana seethed, moving her eyes close to his. "If any mobs come out of this, you're going to be blamed. But I will tell you this . . . Only the mobs will drive us off my property — not you and not Joseph!"

"Let me talk sense into Alpheas! Where's he at?"

"He'll be here in the morning and you're not going to disturb him before then! We're making our wedding plans for this spring." She beheld Porter dumbstruck. "Porter, you knew we were getting married. And Alpheas will not see you in the morning or any other time without Marshal Greene hauling you away for hounding us!"

Porter walked away, still speechless. He was not prepared for news of a marriage this soon. Nor was he willing to subject his children to any more scenes like last time, when he shoved Cutler into the mud. He would have to think out his options to save his kids . . .

CHAPTER 40

The night of June 22, 1844 offered a starlit canopy over the Mississippi River as Porter rowed an old leaky rowboat. Meanwhile Joseph, Hyrum, and Willard Richards bailed water out with their hats.

"Porter," said Joseph, "you must have found the worst boat in Illinois."

They chuckled, and in silence made their way across the shining, star-lit water.

After a few minutes Joseph mumbled:

"That's the hardest thing I ever did."

"What's that?" said Hyrum.

"Leaving Emma and the children."

"They'll join us soon enough."

They were hopeful to have their families join them across the river soon, but first had to establish a camp and find larger boats.

Porter, meanwhile, was distraught over his children, especially Emily. And was torn over what to do.

They pulled their craft ashore and were safely in Montrose, Iowa. Walking quietly through the streets they arrived at the home of William Jordan, a trustworthy friend who gave them shelter and fed them. Joseph explained to him their plans, then turned to Porter:

"Going to be a long walk to the Rocky Mountains unless we have horses. Porter, you might prepare a few and bring them across on the barge tomorrow."

At the Mansion House Porter gathered the horses. Meanwhile his dog Ugly barked at Emma Smith. She stood flustered beside the corral gate with Reynolds Cahoon, a tall, stout, robust fellow whom Porter regarded as *nouveau riche*. Emma turned to Porter, regaining her poise:

"I insist you take Reynolds Cahoon back across the river," she said. "He has a letter for Joseph I want delivered."

"I can deliver it as good as him," said Porter. "So you can stay here, Cahoon."

"I insist, Porter," said Emma, "or I'll see you will not leave this city with my property. Those horses stay or you will take Reynolds Cahoon."

"With all due respect, Emma, I'm not sure you can stop me."

"I'll get word to the ferryman that those horses are my property. And that essentially makes you a thief."

"I guess it does, don't it?"

Porter walked away with the four horses, his dog following. He ordered his dog to quit barking and it obeyed.

Joseph's attornies, H. T. Reid and James Woods, objected.

Thirteen of the men were then released on bail. Suddenly the judge — who was the only magistrate who could grant subpoenas for witnesses — inexplicably disappeared.

Joseph and Hyrum, still under arrest, were marched back to their hotel while several friends joined them. Those who were released on bail rode back to Nauvoo through the rampaging mob.

At 8 PM, as Joseph, Hyrum, and seven friends sat in Joseph's hotel room, the constable suddenly arrived and insisted Joseph and Hyrum go to the Carthage Jail. Looking out the window at the broiling mob, Joseph's two lawyers demanded the prisoners first be brought before a justice of the peace for examination. "They are entitled to this before they can be sent to jail," shouted Joseph's head attorney, Woods. "It's the law!"

The constable then pulled out an illegal mittimus, signed by the judge. Woods dashed to Ford's room to complain of it and to ask for assistance. "Look what is happening here, Governor. In the name of heaven, please intervene."

"I'm afraid I'll have to wash my hands of this matter, sir. I cannot interfere."

The constable, now free to take Joseph and Hyrum from the safety of the hotel, forced them out into the swarm, many of whose participants seemed drunk on both anger and liquor in the hot summer evening air. And there the mob followed Joseph, Hyrum, and seven of their friends — Richards, Taylor, Greene, Markham, Jones, Southwick, and Wasson

— down Walnut Street. Willard Richards and John Taylor pounded their canes onto occasional drunks who tried grabbing them. Wasson was the same who had accompanied Reynolds Cahoon to Montrose days earlier to dissuade Joseph from fleeing West, but now was displaying a turnabout loyalty and courage by staying at his leader's side. Cahoon also revealed such qualities by coming into Carthage the day previously on Joseph's behalf.

The jailer and 20 accompanying state militia barely got them safely through the frenzy and into Carthage Jail.

Inside the doorway Joseph leaned against the two and a half foot thick wall and sighed with both relief and consternation at the fact they were now officially sitting ducks.

Across the street, Frank Worrell cleaned his gun. He eyed Joseph just inside the jailhouse entry, as the massive oak door was slammed shut and locked.

CHAPTER 45

Rockwell and Redden sat in the Warsaw tavern with Emily, and, in the darkness of a setting sun and too few candles, overheard more news that chilled them:

A few rowdies with liquor under their tongues were spouting off something about a celebration party they'd enjoy after attacking Nauvoo the next night. Porter gazed at Redden. Both men were stunned. They quietly took their bottle with them and, as Porter grasped Emily's hand, they shot quickly out the door.

Riding at a gallop in Redden's wagon for Nauvoo, the two quickly searched for a strategy:

"We can't go after Joseph yet!" yelled Porter.

"If we don't, who'll save him?" argued Redden.

"You think if we busted him out of jail while our city was put to ashes he'd even talk to us again?"

"How do you know what he'll think?" said Redden louder.

"I know him! Can't you see the look in his eyes if he was already protected by the state militia — and here we are takin' him away — only to ride into Nauvoo to find half our neighbors being massacred?"

"So what do you wanna do!"

"Only thing we can!" shouted Porter.

Their wagon wheels shot up dust on the dry summer dirt road leading to Nauvoo. After a silence, Porter muttered:

"Then we'll set out for Carthage — but only after we take care of the mob marching on Nauvoo."

Emily meanwhile, overhearing this talk, became moment by moment increasingly afraid for her brothers and sisters. Talk of war — right in their own neighborhood? She shivered harder than she could remember.

The next evening at eight, Joseph and Hyrum were still in Carthage Jail. Their two attorneys arrived and spoke with John Greene, Nauvoo's city marshal. Woods stood at the window a moment then turned to face Joseph: "Ford has met with his officers and decided to leave for Nauvoo tomorrow morning at eight."

Joseph relaxed. "Good, we'll be safely back in Nauvoo then."

"That's just it," said Woods. "He's changed his mind. He's not taking you with him. And he's leaving 50 militiamen as guard — but I don't know which militia they're from. The Carthage Greys would kill you."

Reid spoke up. "The news gets worse, Joseph. The judge has decided to postpone the return of subpoenas another two days."

Joseph spoke incredulously, "Saturday? We're holed up here till Saturday?"

Reid continued, "The judge consulted with no one about it."

Joseph's news would worsen. His uncle, John Smith, would be visiting Almon Babbitt in nearby Macedonia that very moment — at 8:15 PM. Joseph wanted Babbitt as an attorney at the trial.

But Babbitt would reply, "You are too late. I am already engaged on the other side."

Perhaps Babbitt's ego was wounded since Joseph had already chosen Woods as his chief attorney. But Babbitt would yet, as a Mormon attorney, serve both Brigham and Porter well. And later, ironically, an incident involving the three of them would alter the course of American history.

Frank Worrell led 70 Carthage Grey militiamen — all out of uniform — and three dozen "good ole boys" from Warsaw towards Nauvoo.

This was the mob force Porter and Redden had heard about, and they now carried torches to use against the temple, Joseph's Mansion House, and other major buildings. Some had tried surreptitiously to locate Porter's hut, but had failed. His current lodgings were a well-guarded secret, known only by city hierarchists.

When the mob reached the outskirts of Nauvoo, they were stunned once again to find Porter at the forefront of a waiting army.

Once again the mob was thwarted.

Once again, Frank Worrell set horseback, angered and frustrated. Glaring at the city defenders led by the notorious

Rockwell, he suddenly waved a white handkerchief and rode forward. Porter also rode forward. He wore buckskins, Worrell wool cloth; both men stopped their horses and glared six feet from each other's eyes.

"Porter, I'm gonna remove your head if you stick it in my trap. That's fair warning."

"Yeah, I'm waiting."

Worrell turned his horse, then stopped a moment.

"I'll tell you something, boy," said Worrell. "When I'm finished with this Smith business, you're next. And I don't care how many men you've got around you."

Porter used every effort to constrain himself from immediately attacking. He glanced back at his band of volunteers — the Nauvoo Legion had been disarmed but several dozen men owned their own weapons and these were the lads who had followed him to the perimeters of the city. He gazed across their faces and knew they were as angry as he. They had been stripped of their weapons, their uniforms, their leader, and their pride, and were now following Porter to not only defend their city but to seek revenge. Yet he knew any violence would instigate harm to Joseph — possibly before he and his fellow defenders could reach Nauvoo to rescue Joseph.

"And if you're thinking of rescuing Joseph," quipped Worrell, "drop the idea. We've got 200 Greys ready to move on you if you boys even show your faces near Carthage."

Worrell looked about Porter's men, half of whom had merely swords and pitchforks, and realized the governor had by now disarmed the Legion. "And our boys," he added, "are armed."

Porter was shocked that Worrell had figured out his strategy and check-mated him.

"You may've got the victory on us tonight, but you will see us take your city yet — your beloved "Kingdom on a Hill." And as for Joseph, he's in our hands to do as we please. But you will guarantee his death by a mob if you even take these boys outside Nauvoo — you got me straight?"

Porter merely stared at Worrell and icily smiled, then turned his horse, and left.

Worrell fumed, then led his off-duty militiamen back into the woods.

As Porter's band of armed volunteers dispersed at Porter's command, he decided to follow Worrell.

An hour later at a campfire ahead he spotted him and stopped. He perceived through the trees Frank Worrell in the moonlight gulping down a bottle of cheap whiskey, then he heard Worrell shout, "Let's take care of business in Carthage!"

Worrell's men whooped and cheered and mounted their horses.

Porter ran to his horse and took off the other direction. He hoped to grab only a handful of his best warriors to sneak into Carthage from the south and storm the jail with explosives — then rescue Joseph before the Greys even knew what hit them!

But as he arrived at Nauvoo, he realized his fighting band had all scattered to their homes across the city. In recent months Joseph's home had become headquarters to their city's leaders, so he galloped to the Mansion House, hoping to find anyone willing to join him.

CHAPTER 46

Back at Carthage jail all was quiet. The upstairs consisted of the jailer's quarters — a comfortable room except for the fact it was upstairs and therefore absorbed the building's heat both winter and summer, including hot June days like this — and also the jail itself — a heavily barred "cage-like" cell in a small-windowed room that held even more heat because of the small, castle-like windows.

The jailer had taken a liking to the five prisoners and for their own safety had placed them in his own upstairs quarters, where they were all asleep. A gunshot rang out. All five jerked awake. Joseph peered out the window and saw nothing. The air again became still. The others — Hyrum, Willard Richards, John Fullmer, and Dan Jones — a short, broad Welshman who was visiting — returned to their sleep.

Joseph laid down again on the floor between Fullmer and Jones and said, "I would like to see my family again. I would to God that I could preach to the Saints in Nauvoo once more."

He turned to Dan Jones, "Are you afraid to die?"

In his Welsh accent Dan replied, "Has that time come, think you?"

Joseph said, "You will yet see Wales, and fulfill the mission appointed you before you die."

Nothing more was said.

Racing his horse to the Mansion House headquarters, Porter arrived, only to find a large contingency of Illinois state militia. Their horses were tied outside with a guard watching. Porter realized he had an excuse to enter: He had earlier left his hat in a conference room upstairs.

"Who's inside?" shouted Porter to the guard outside.

"Governor Ford and some officers."

Porter went to the door.

"I'm afraid you can't go in," said the guard.

"I left my hat here — and I'm afraid nobody's stopping me."

The guard pulled a pistol. "I'd hate to use this."

"And I'd hate to see you die trying."

The guard studied him, placing his pistol to Porter's chest.

Porter said, "Even if you got me in the heart, I'd get a good clean shot off. I'm a tough old devil," he smiled. "We'd both be dead."

The guard studied Porter's eyes, lowered his weapon, and finally nodded him inside. "First, hand me your pistol." Porter did so and entered the house. He climbed the stairs past boisterous officers and civilian staff to his left and right in both parlors.

In an upper room to his right he spotted his hat. As he

walked in to grab it he noticed a room full of men in suits sitting and listening quietly to a speaker standing at a table. As the speaker checked his pocket watch he said, "The deed is done before this time." Porter then noticed Governor Ford, who was checking his own pocket watch when he looked up and saw Porter. Their eyes met and held.

The room suddenly fell silent as all eyes turned to Porter Rockwell.

He was stunned.

Without a word, he grabbed his hat and ran down the stairs.

A militia captain jumped from his chair, ready to order a dispatch to stop the notorious outlaw, but Governor Ford placed his hand on the captain's shoulder and shook his head no. He did not want to escalate the violence he was certain that was about to occur, nor did he want his name politically attached to any part of it.

The captain stared at the governor a moment, and finally sat back down.

CHAPTER 47

Outside the Mansion House, Porter grabbed his gun from the guard, quickly re-mounted, and rode up Water Street. He passed Gilbert Belnap, a loyal, carefree chap whom Porter knew could be called upon for anything at a moment's notice. He was the only possible recruit in sight — the only rough sort among the farmers and tradesman he could see on the street — and Porter's excitement was catching. He stopped Belnap and told him he had all the guns the two of them would need; all he needed was Belnap's answer.

Belnap's eyes dilated and he turned his horse around. Both men took off in a gallop towards Browning's Gun Shop where they told Jonathon of their plan, and received a few bags of powder they could stuff into miniature barrels with fuses he then handed them which would blow away any jail door. Porter and Belnap quickly tied down the "barrels" and took off in a gallop toward Parleys Street, then up the hill and southeasterward towards Carthage, ready to sneak attack the jail, rescue Joseph, and take on 200 Carthage Greys, if necessary.

At Carthage Jail, Joseph and his friends sat talking peace-fully, with no idea of the plans being laid across town — in both cities. John Fullmer had left earlier that day and been replaced by John Taylor, who like Porter was one of Joseph's most trusted few. All four friends who were with Joseph were in fact those he would have most readily given his life for, as well as for Por-ter. Also engaged in friendly cnversation with them was a guard, who turned to leave their room when, at the top of the stairs, someone below summoned him two or three times. The guard went down and Joseph heard a little rustling at the door. His breathing became uneasy.

All six of Joseph's official guards were now outside facing a mob of a hundred men painted with blackened faces. The sight shook them. Most of the mob were off-duty Carthage Greys led by Frank Worrell, and they began screaming like Indians. They shouted to the guards to surrender. From their large room Willard Richards looked out the window and saw them by the front door. He heard another hundred around the building. The six guards fired three or four warning shots over their heads, but were quickly pushed aside.

As the mob rushed up the stairs, Joseph sprang to his coat and grabbed a hidden revolver, brought to him earlier by friend Cyrus Wheelock. Hyrum went for his pistol and Taylor and Richards for their canes.

All sprang to the door and braced themselves against it. Soon they heard the first gunshot down the stairway. The ball smashed through the wood. Joseph, Richards and Taylor jumped to the left and Hyrum dashed back in front of the door to keep it shut. Several in the mob leaped against the door — it was cracked open and barrels were stuck through the opening. Richards and Taylor, holding their canes, beat away the barrels as best they could, but several weapons from the mobbers were fired.

Joseph reached around the door with his six-shooter pepper revolver and fired, but two or three barrels mis-fired, although he managed to wound several attackers.

Hyrum fired his pistol, then was shot in the face — a ball struck him in the left side of his nose. Several other shots hit his chest, side, and leg, then he collapsed.

Joseph knelt beside him, held his head, and watched him die.

Taylor sprang to the east window to jump — but was shot. Now on the floor, he rolled under the bed, nursing his wound, when another flurry of shots came from the doorway and penetrated his body, hitting his watch and stopping it at 5:16. Willard Richards meanwhile backed against the wall, unscathed. Joseph gave both Taylor and Richards a glance, then in order to draw attention away from his friends he dropped his pistol on the floor and leaped into the window. Several pistol shots came from the doorway. Two shots hit him in the back. As he spun, another hit him in the right collar bone.

From the well below, one man aimed his rifle directly at Joseph's chest — and fired.

Blood shot from him. Several more shots came and Joseph toppled through the window. He exclaimed, "Oh Lord, my God," and fell to the ground.

The mob shouted and cheered as they gathered around him.

Under the overcast sky they watched him die. Then, a still-ness fell over them. All stood around him like white oaks in a windless forest.

(Author's note: From all recorded sources, every detail of this scene was included.)

Frank Worrell would later claim to be among those who had attacked and shot Joseph.

Six miles outside town, as they rode toward Carthage, Por-ter and Gilbert Belnap noticed a wagon team coming high speed from a hundred yards away.

A quarter mile beyond the wagon were a dozen galloping horsemen. Porter recognized the wagon driver, George D. Grant, who shouted:

"They're chasing me — head to Nauvoo!"

Porter and Gilbert galloped alongside the wagon and Por-ter yelled, "What about Joseph?"

"He's dead!" Grant snapped his reins and the horses quickly regained speed.

Porter glowered at the on-coming horsemen. His compan-ion, Belnap, saw Porter take from his saddlebags three weap-ons and hand one to him. Then immediately they heard from a hundred yards ahead, gunshots . . .

George Grant yelled from his wagon back to Porter, still standing in the road, "C'mon! there's a dozen of 'em!"

But from Porter's expression, his companion, Belnap, knew there was no turning back.

They were poised for war . . . two against 12.

CHAPTER 48

Gilbert Belnap leaped behind a tree for cover. Porter, however, stood in the road and simply stared at the on-coming mob.

The horsemen opened fire.

Balls whistled about Porter. No shots struck him, though he was a wide-open target.

Belnap, safely behind the tree, watched in amazement as his companion lowered his revolver . . . and fired. A horseman flew off his horse and crashed to the mud. Porter squeezed off another shot. A second horseman was hit in the shoulder and his gun flew away. Porter fired twice more. Two other horsemen were slung off their horses by the impact of flying lead.

The remaining horsemen came to a halt; they aimed and fired. Mud splattered beside Porter, but no shots hit him.

He stepped to his saddlebag and took another revolver. Balls continued hitting around him, ricocheting off trees and whistling over Belnap's head. Porter, holding two revolvers now, took aim and fired one shot with his first revolver, then with his second — and two men were shot off their saddles, crashing to the mud. Another had a rifle shot out of his hand. Another flipped out of his saddle in a somersault.

The remaining horsemen stopped in their saddles and all stared in wonder. One glanced at the others behind him and suddenly they all made a silent, single decision: They took off galloping in retreat.

Belnap grabbed his hat and waved it in the air shouting, exultant to be alive. But Porter stared off in anguish. He took one last shot and a horseman flew from his horse, wrapping his neck around a tree limb.

Porter lowered his head. He mounted his horse and rode away slowly, leaving Gilbert Belnap standing in the road a moment, staring blankly at him, in awe.

On the ride home with Belnap, who had momentarily caught up with him, Porter recalled his most recent days with Joseph. He wondered what he could have done. Should've done. His mind soared back to his earliest years, with Joseph, playing in the woodlands of Manchester, New York as youngsters.

Porter and Gilbert Belnap arrived at Parley Street and made their way to the edge of the bluff overlooking "the flats." They stopped their horses and gazed over the city. They beheld their people walking and riding on the streets. The citizens of Nauvoo did not know of Joseph and Hyrum yet, because three miles outside Nauvoo, George Grant — the wagon driver who had told Porter of the news — had been stopped by Governor Ford and his militia and prevented from reaching Nauvoo. Minutes earlier, when Porter had caught Ford in the Mansion House talking about Joseph's death, Ford had panicked. He and the state militia had run to their horses and galloped away from Nauvoo, fearing Porter would start an uprising. On the way to Carthage, Ford had come across George Grant and another Mormon and taken them under military force back to Grant's house, 1½ miles east of Carthage. Ford had done this to buy himself time, also wishing to flee his headquarters at Carthage now, fearing a Mormon attack.

Business was unusually heavy that day and pedestrians and wagons packed the roads. Crowds were anxious to hear word from Carthage, and when they spotted the two men on horseback coming down the road on Parley Street, they assumed they had news for the city. When they beheld it was Porter they were certain their beloved leader, Joseph, would be arriving behind him on the woodland road any moment.

In their faces Porter could see their optimistic expectations: They were waiting for the Prophet to appear from over the bluff on horseback as he had countless times before when freed from jails and judges and court proceedings.

Porter halted his horse on the road and stared at them. Much of the city seemed to be near Parley Street that day, and he felt a sudden sullenness descend on the town. The entire city seemed to feel it. Dozens inexplicably took notice of him. Hundreds of others slowed or stopped on nearby roads, and then it strangely seemed as though all the city turned its eyes to him.

By his demeanor, they knew what had happened.

CHAPTER 49

The next day, June 28, 1844, on Porter's 31st birthday, at 2:30 PM, Porter stood motionless with his daughter Emily among 12,000 Nauvoo citizens as Joseph's and Hyrum's bodies were driven through town on two separate wagons, driven by Joseph's brother Samuel and Artois Hamilton, owner of the Hamilton House hotel where the bodies had been taken the night before and had spent the evening in rough coffins. Escorting the two drivers was a guard of eight state militia detached by General Deming. The front of the crowd began a mile east of the temple, and from there the mourners followed the wagon on Mulholland Street and then south to the Mansion House. Riding on one of the wagons was Willard Richards, who had not only survived the attack but had miraculously escaped all harm, with not even a scratch, as Joseph had prophesied he would. Meanwhile, John Taylor had been brought to the city earlier, wounded.

Porter had retrieved Emily the evening before from her

home, and she'd spent the night at his cabin. She had found in him a strange intensity, and it saddened her. Especially disconcerting was the fact he would not answer her questions, although she did understand the reason.

As the clopping of the horses' feet echoed onto the crowded, quiet street, Porter surveyed the poignant sight — the wagons moved slowly past him, revealing Joseph and Hyrum. Joseph's eyes were closed and he looked peaceful. Porter gazed at him, appreciating his only close friend in the world, one last time. He then noticed young Joseph III across the street standing with his brothers and sisters, weeping beside Emma, who, five months pregnant, seemed in a state of shock.

Porter turned his head.

The next day, June 29, 1844, ironically the day that had been appointed for Joseph's trial wherein dozens of witnesses had been lined up to clear him, he and Hyrum lay in state at the Mansion House from 8 AM to 5 PM, allowing 20,000 visitors to see them one last time.

Porter and Emily were the last to leave the Mansion House.

Thomas Sharp meanwhile wrote at his desk in Warsaw, Illinois (author's note: The following paragraph was the actual text):

"Because of Joseph's and Hyrum's outrages on the rights of our citizens, the killing of the Smiths, which was performed by our most respectable citizens, was justified, and the act ought to have been done and the perpetrators will not only be protected but honored."

The epitaph was going in that day's edition. Moments later Sharp received news that two more of the mob that had attacked Porter on the Carthage Road two days earlier had just died from their gunshot wounds, and suddenly his face twitched. On the front page he now announced, "The rise of a new despot in our midst — the one next needing our most immediate attention: the man we need to crush without delay — the Avenging Angel himself — Porter Rockwell!"

PART III

Fraternity

CHAPTER 50

Porter stood among thousands, listening to church official Sidney Rigdon addressing the people of Nauvoo. The point of his discourse was well-taken: Rigdon was Joseph's only surviving council member and therefore deserved the reins to the kingdom.

Porter disliked him. He knew Joseph had sought to release the ever-aspiring, sometimes ingratiating Rigdon from leadership, but for months the Mormons as a body had not allowed it: They had literally refused to sustain Joseph on this issue when he had brought the matter to a vote.

"So here he is," thought Porter to himself, "without the Council of the Twelve to keep an eye on him. And he is trying to take over as president of the church." Porter felt like taking the platform himself and telling them what he thought. Unfortunately, he was regarded as not just a protector of prophets but as a bonified ruffian, so he held his peace.

Unknown to Rigdon — or at least conveniently overlooked by him — the leadership of the church now lay in the hands of the Twelve Apostles. And none of them were yet in Nauvoo — though they had all been summoned from their missions by a church clerk writing them in the Eastern U.S., informing them of Joseph's death and urging them to return to settle the matter of who should be president. Individually, many of the Twelve had reaped a broad harvest in England and were now on the East coast returning with thousands of converts who would add strength to their kingdom.

A majority of the Twelve, including Brigham Young, returned in the nick of time before Rigdon could take power. On August 8, 1844 a sizeable crowd in Nauvoo saw Brigham stand at the podium and deliver a most unusual sermon. Anson Call, George Cannon and others reported later in their diaries they saw Brigham take on both the appearance and the voice of Joseph Smith.

Brigham was chosen the new leader, not necessarily from the heavenly "sign," but from his seniority in the Council of the Twelve. He was stocky, square-jawed, and to some resembled a bull dog with a continual smile in his eyes.

Porter was pleased with his new leader. Brigham had taken two years himself to convert to the church, and had always been considered a methodical, bold, likeable, sometimes tactless, but nevertheless never-wavering Apostle . . . and now he would be king.

Brigham did not care much for small talk and he was not given to general reflections. That's why he liked Porter, and felt he could comfortably confide in him. Brigham immediately sent a messenger to dispatch Porter. When he arrived minutes later, he sat before the venerable young prophet and folded his arms. It made him rather uncomfortable knowing he was being assessed, but Brigham liked what he saw.

Porter admired Brigham in return, but did not have the same rapport with him he had enjoyed with Joseph and Hyrum. Nor had he spent a thousandth as many hours with him. He wasn't sure he wanted to. Brigham seemed satisfied keeping their relationship a bit on the formal side. He could sense Brigham trusted him implicitly, but their natural flow of conversation usually ended with Brigham's first words, "Good morning." In essence, Brigham had his own close friends.

At Joseph's death, Porter had immediately moved out of the Mansion House and back to his mother's. There, Ugly was joyous to see him every day.

However, Porter's depression over his friend's death led him often to his secret place next to the woods — his secret garden spot where he enjoyed tending his small garden. Because of recent events, he decided to now build a woodland cabin even deeper in the woods, concealed from all roads and houses, yet only a hundred yards from his garden. There, he could sleep and live and even bring his children, mother and siblings if events caused the safety of the city to collapse.

But what happened next took him by surprise — especially with the speed at which it unfolded. Brigham soon learned that local mobbers planned "wolf hunts" — just like in Missouri — to burn out rural farms of church members. He reacted by rearming the Nauvoo Legion with a few weapons they could round up, and calling for drills.

Thomas Sharp used that news as fuel to fire up the locals in his paper and to take it a step further: He wrote a new article claiming Brigham planned to use the Nauvoo Legion to attack them — unless they attacked first!

CHAPTER 51

Hundreds of locals gathered and marched on Mormon farms in rural Hancock County. Since those saints were vulnerable on isolated farms, they fled their homes and took their march upon the muddy roads leading to Nauvoo, penniless and without possessions. The mob, led by Frank Worrell, decided to continue its onslaught and attack the city itself, but they were halted on a country road by Brigadier General J. J. Hardin and 500 non-Mormon allies, determined to protect Nauvoo.

As the two armies converged on each other, ready for battle, Frank Worrell walked up to General Hardin and spat at his feet.

"You plan a little trouble, Worrell?" said the general.

"No, sir, I plan to straighten out a little trouble."

"And what trouble do you speak of?"

"The Mormons are the trouble," said Worrell. "If you join us we'll free ourselves of the trouble."

Hardin smiled, "I suppose you mean that." He lit his pipe casually. "But if you take another step forward, your troubles will just begin."

Worrell squinted at him, suddenly intimidated by Hardin's calm confidence. He realized he was being defeated once again, and it only added to his resolve to smash Porter for good.

When Frank Worrell reported the incident to Thomas Sharp, the editor smiled.

"What're you smiling at?" shouted Worrell.

"We'll simply put a better plan into effect — one that will just plain impassion the populace like the good general has never before seen — and then I believe even he will hop aboard for the ride . . ."

Worrell looked at him curiously.

"You'll see soon enough," said Sharp, answering his silent question. "But first I want you to make sure my paper gets in the hands of the *Burlington Hawkeye,* the *Iowa Patriot,* the *Alton Telegraph,* and the *Quincy Whig.* 'Clear?"

Brigham held up several newspapers as he spoke to a crowd of saints in Nauvoo:

"Outsiders and lowbrows have invaded our city. They've begun thieving against Mormons and non-Mormons alike, but Thomas Sharp's newspaper and now all the others claim we are the ones committing the crimes. And," he added, turning to Porter, "these newspapers claim Porter here is the leader of the thieves."

Porter, standing in the crowd, was amused. "I may be a devil but I ain't no thief."

The crowd chuckled.

Brigham nodded. "My guess is, if you're sighted outside the county, you'll be shot on the spot."

"Does that mean you want me to leave the county with my tail between my legs?" joked Porter.

The crowd laughed harder.

"So what does General Hardin think of all this?" said Gilbert Belnap, standing beside Porter.

"He has finally turned against us," said Brigham, "as well as his 500 man militia that volunteered to protect us. So I think it's time we can stop smiling."

The next morning Porter slept soundly. He heard twigs snapping outside. His sixth sense rang an alarm and he jumped out of bed. But before he could grab his pistol, the door burst open, and there stood one of the most unexpected sights he had ever beheld. Sheriff Reynolds of Independence, Missouri holding two pistols, backed up by four deputies outside, surrounding the cabin, and two others right behind him. Reynolds cocked his weapon and smiled.

"So how'd you find me, old friend?" said Porter, raising his hands to surrender.

CHAPTER 52

Ugly came ambling in.

"So that's it," mumbled Porter. "That's how you found me. You took him from Ma's house and sent him after me. You're one sharp sheriff, Reynolds," said Porter. "But I do believe you're in my territory now, so you may be up against your match."

"What's the matter, Rockwell, will this make you look foolish to the press when they get wind of it — using your own dog against you?" Reynolds chuckled.

"We'll see who looks foolish," mumbled Porter.

Sheriff Reynolds then stepped deeper into Porter's woodland cabin with both guns raised.

Porter suddenly lunged from behind the door and shoved Reynolds into his two deputies. He spotted the sheriff's gun on the floor and grabbed it. He turned the gun onto the three men, and nodded them outside.

Using Reynolds as cover, Porter made his way slowly from the cabin to his horse, tied near the sheriff's and deputies' horses. He smacked the lawmen's horses and they all scattered. He then took his own horse and held his pistol on the sheriff.

The other four deputies converged on the scene. They hid behind trees and took aim.

"You shoot and this trigger is pulled," said Porter. He walked with Reynolds and his horse deep into the woods. After a half hour they stopped.

"I reckon this is far enough," said Porter, who mounted up. "You don't mind if I borrow your gun, do you?" he chortled. He then ordered Reynolds to remove his boots and hand them over, so the lawman could not return to his posse just too awfully quickly.

Porter rode away, leaving the sheriff to walk barefoot back to his men — gunless, bootless, and horseless — muttering dark oaths under his breath.

That afternoon, with his horse drinking, Porter sat at a stream and heard distant dogs barking.

Suddenly, several yards from him, three possemen stepped out of the brush. He met their eyes. He glanced at his horse — it was too far from him. He darted into the woods. Several gunshots trailed, and he smacked the horse to escape safely in another direction.

Through the woods he ran. The possemen took after him. But within minutes they lost him. He eventually came to thick trees and stopped. He panted and heard the other search party — the one with dogs — coming closer. He took off again, and soon came to a creek.

He splashed into it and ran upstream. When the dogs arrived, they lost his scent.

A hundred yards back, the lead horseman spotted him running in shallow water and disappearing around a bend.

Porter ran breathlessly. He heard the dogs barking louder, closer. His foot caught a rock and he stumbled. He struggled his way to his feet and resumed running in the creek.

Across a dark green meadow he ran, arriving at thick woods.

The dogs, horses, and possemen all kept pace, and they soon arrived at the same woods. There, the dogs stopped and yapped, apparently trapping their prey. The horsemen dismounted and surrounded an object.

Protruding out of thick brush were Porter's feet, his boots barely visible.

The possemen glanced at one another, satisfied. Reynolds stepped forward and bellowed:

"Come out, Rockwell."

No movement from their victim. Figuring him too stubborn for his own good, they began threatening and swearing at him. Sheriff Reynolds then recalled the humiliation Porter had forced upon him right before his men — all after he had once had the desperado right in his grasp in Independence Jail.

"One last chance, Rockwell," yelled Reynolds.

No response.

So the sheriff smiled and bellowed to his posse, "All right, boys, open fire!"

They commenced firing into the form, expending more than enough rounds to kill a dozen men.

A deputy whacked away at the weeds to inspect the corpse, and finally exposed it — first its trousers, then its belt, and finally they saw what they had shot to ribbons:

Porter's clothes, stuffed with weeds.

CHAPTER 53

The real Porter Rockwell swam in long johns. A half mile downstream he emerged from a river, exhausted, but chuckling, hearing all the gunshots, and then the shouting and cursing from Sheriff Reynolds.

He soon staggered ashore and began walking. He strode as fast as his lungs would allow. The sun beamed through tall trees and a warm breeze cooled his wet clothes. Birds chirped peacefully, and he finally came to a woodland cabin.

There he beheld, standing in the framework of the open door, the figure of a young girl about his daughter's age. She backed into the house and squinted at his wet, ill-fitting long johns.

He was the first to break the strained silence.

"Ain't you gonna invite me in?" said he.

They stared at one another fully fifteen seconds.

Finally, she mumbled, "'Wanna come in?"

Inside at the dinner table he sat, eating like a bear. He shoveled the food into his mouth in enormous mouthfuls. The young girl studied his large hairy neck and arms. The thought crossed her mind that his blue eyes sparkled like gems. He was an interesting character.

"Ain't you ever seen a man in his underwear?" he said.

She smiled, and he kept eating. The banquet before him consisted of thick chowder, freshly-churned butter and warm bread.

"You have some nerve," she said.

"Some nerve, eh? What do you mean some nerve? You think I always enter strangers' homes in my underwear? That's more than some nerve. Give me credit, little girl."

"You think I'm little? I'm 16."

"Well, you're a real grown-up, then," he muttered dryly. She was in fact a few years older than Emily, although she looked younger.

"Do you do this often?" she said with a smile behind her question.

"Every chance I get."

Despite his demeanor she perceived he was, deep down, very embarrassed. She studied him in silence a minute.

"Where're your folks?" he said.

"Getting supplies in town."

"Tell them I appreciate your kindness."

She smiled, charmed by this strange-looking, bear-like fellow.

"I reckon I better be on my way," he said, finishing the meal and rising.

"Wait." She disappeared to the back room and returned with a wool blanket. He took it and draped it over himself.

"Just don't go anywhere public," she said with a twinkle, then giggled. The bubble in her laughter was the kind that made you want to laugh, too.

"How long 'you been married?" he said.

She laughed harder, enjoying his teasing. "Ain't married."

He figured she'd make a fine friend for Emily, despite the small age difference.

"Get your things, little girl. We've gotta find your folks. Grab your best possessions — you won't see this farm again."

She hastily packed family jewelry and small heirlooms into a saddlebag, then with Porter's assistance herded off the family cow towards town. She and Porter waked as fast as they could, and on the outskirts of town found her parents.

"Mary Ann!" cried Mary Neff, her mother. "What're you doing here?"

"What's he doing with my clothes on?" said John Neff. "And how come you've got the cow!"

"You can stay at my ma's," said Porter to the family.

"What the devil are you talking about?" said Mary Neff.

"Walk with me," said Porter. "But don't look back. Your farm won't be there by morning."

At Green Plains, Illinois that same night, Frank Worrell stood with a crowd of angry citizens, listening and watching by torch-light to an impassioned preacher:

"Why can't the Avenging Angel just get caught once and for good? I ask you — is it the power of the devil that supports him? I say we show his people what happens when they don't cooperate with the law!"

Gunshots suddenly shattered the air. Two horsemen galloped past and fired again. Balls whistled over the speaker, but no one was hit.

Nevertheless, the signal was clear to those gathered: Brigham was fighting back . . . and, as Frank Worrell now shouted to the group, "If ever a war has been declared, this is it!"

CHAPTER 54

At the Mansion House Brigham Young confided to his aides: "The affair at Green Plains last night was staged by *agent provocateurs*. Our people had no part in the shooting. Our enemies staged it because Porter escaped them and made them even angrier. Now they have to get back at us by riling up our neighbors even further." He reported to his aides Porter's escape from the Missouri sheriff, and chuckled at the clever escape from the bloodhounds and taking the sheriff's gun away from him; he had learned all this from Sheriff Reynolds himself after the event, as the good sheriff had wanted to be reimbursed by Brigham for the stolen pistol and boots; whereupon Brigham had merely smiled at him. Now, while Brigham admired Porter's antics, he simultaneously wondered just how any single human being could frustrate his enemies so thoroughly that it could get them all into so much doggone trouble. He nevertheless smiled again when he thought of how Porter had escaped the sheriff and made a mockery of him in front of his roughnecked, prejudiced posse. "Darn, I wish I had had seen it."

With the posse gone back to Missouri, Porter figured it safe to return to his woodland home.

Brigham meanwhile had found a hut beside town for the Neffs, since they wanted privacy and a place for their cow, although they gratefully acknowledged Porter's mother, Sarah Rockwell, for putting them up several days with such hospitality.

Porter moved along the trees in the shadows of dawn and arrived at his concealed cabin. Ugly strutted up, wagging his tail. The dog was his finest friend.

"Next time," said Porter, "don't announce to the whole world where I live. All right?"

Ugly wagged his monstrous tail.

The next morning Porter was awakened by raucous, cacophonous crowing. He stood, amazed to see several hundred birds descending on the woodland grove; then, as suddenly as the birds had appeared, they left, flapping their large black wings and cawing.

Although tired, he was now fully awake. The forest's rich odors filled his lungs. Ugly panted in his face, wanting breakfast.

"Go over to the Mansion House and pant in Emma's face," said Porter. "She'll feed you."

He watched Ugly amble down the road to visit Emma at the Mansion House, and smiled.

———————

Emma was chagrined at seeing Ugly pawing on her front door. While she did not allow animals into her home anymore, Joseph had demanded Porter's dog be an exception — for a reason she did not fully understand. Despite her later requests to the contrary, the animal had free reign of the place, and she still honored Joseph's wish, even after the disastrous brush with her closet years earlier at Far West.

The dog feasted at the Mansion House, and Emma watched and listened to the animal eat loudly on her kitchen floor, nauseating her.

Soon Porter arrived there to retrieve both his dog and his last belongings. Meanwhile, Brigham and other leaders had made their headquarters down the road away from the Mansion House at his own home's added east wing, respecting both Emma's privacy and her nosiness. While he admired her endurance over the years, he did not care for her increasing confrontations. She was vying for church leadership to be handed to her sons. Not possessing the same glow she had in earlier years, and no longer attending church services, she seemed to Porter merely a shadow of the woman he once knew. And it was evident now from her incessant criticisms of Brigham and other leaders that she would not remain in the fold. Porter quickly left with his dog to visit Brigham.

A half mile downroad he realized he had left a cache of ammo at the Mansion House; he and Ugly returned to retrieve it.

When he had an hour earlier announced to Emma that he was leaving and taking the dog with him, she had beamed. But as she now observed them both out the parlor window, returning, she slunk into her bedroom, not able to bear smelling either creature at close range again.

Porter dismounted and walked with Ugly to the front door. Joseph's oldest boy, Joseph III, passed them, studied the animal, and muttered to Porter, "He sure is an ugly critter."

Porter thanked him and continued into the house.

"Tell your mama I'm just getting my last things. She's welcome to say goodbye to my dog again if she wishes." He smiled.

Joseph III smiled back and left the room to tell her.

CHAPTER 55

With his belongings, Porter set off to see Brigham. He found the new prophet cleaning up recent construction efforts on Joseph's "Nauvoo House," one block north from the newer Mansion House. The Nauvoo House served as a gigantic hotel, with two wings of 120 feet each, a depth of 40 feet, and a planned height of three stories.

Joseph had received a revelation as recorded in the LDS Doctrine and Covenants, a book of modern scripture, section 124 (and RLDS section 107) to build the Nauvoo House in order to provide hotel rooms for visitors. In February 1841 a committee had been formed to oversee its construction. Its estimated cost was $150,000 and the Mormons decided to issue stock to finance construction. Joseph had donated the land for the structure, and for that he and his descendants were to receive rooms for their on-going residency. In October 1841 Joseph had placed the manuscript of the *Book of Mormon* in the cornerstone of the building. More recently

Joseph's and Hyrum's bodies had been secretly buried there to protect them from mob enemies before being placed at the family cemetery directly across the street. Work on the building's expansion had progressed spottily due to a lack of funds, although a recent push on August 18, 1845 had involved a number of workers to try to finish the structure. Shortly afterwards, construction on the building had ceased altogether in order to finish the temple, but Brigham knew that in coming months the walls of the Nauvoo House would reach the second floor — even if it were never finished. This optimistic planning was due to a peculiar but healthy outlook, according to some, for the Mormons to always remain working on projects for the public good — as though nothing were wrong — even when their proverbial walls were collapsing about them.

On this day Porter found Brigham picking up chunks of sawed, left-over boards and hauling them to a pile. Brigham smiled upon seeing him and handed him half his armload of boards for him to carry. As they walked, Brigham cleared his throat, "Where've you been?"

"I've been busy," smiled Porter.

Groveled Brigham, "That's what I'm always afraid of."

"So what assignment do you have for me?"

Brigham was again pleased with Porter's specific, to-the-point topic.

"I'll tell you what's happened since yesterday. A hundred families were burned out of their homes last night in the southern part of the county. I need you and Brother Redden to gather them here to the city. We'll find places for them to stay — and even this half-completed hotel might work for a few rooms." Brigham then explained further what had happened:

Two major Mormon communities, Lima and Morley's Settlement, had been attacked two days earlier on September 10, 1845. Morley's Settlement was also known as Yelrome — a designation spelled backwards with an extra "e" — and founded in 1839 by Isaac Morley, three miles northeast of Lima, Adams County and 25 miles south of Nauvoo. As the home of Alpheas Cutler — Luana's new love — and almost 425 others, they were vulnerable to mob action, being so far from Nauvoo. On this date, buildings were burned and the children of Edmund Durfee were shot at but missed. On November 15, the mob would shoot to death Durfee himself, and soon the Mormon village would lay in ashes, abandoned by its inhabitants fleeing to the comparative safety of Nauvoo.

The other significant Mormon community this far south was Lima, Illinois, important to Nauvoo because of its agricultural activity. Church leaders were afraid both the town and its crops would be destroyed. Their fear was based on the fact Lima was located between Warsaw, home of Thomas Sharp (who had not only spear-headed anti-Mormon press but had actually organized the Anti-Mormon Party in 1841), and Quincy, 43 miles south of Nauvoo and the home of another large anti-Mormon Party established just recently, in fact by the summer of 1845.

Brigham had just learned of the attack on Lima — and the burning of houses there — the previous morning — on September 11, 1845. He, John Taylor and others had then met and decided to send word to the surrounding settlements to come to Nauvoo with their grain. They also had decided among themselves to work faster and harder at completing the temple in order to receive their "endowments" — special ordinances and instruction from the Lord, rather than "to squabble," as John Taylor had put it, "with the mob about property, seeing that the houses were not much importance." Porter now heard Brigham's report of all this and found Taylor's perception of property downright refreshing compared to Emma's earlier proclamation which had held back Joseph from going West, and which eventually of course had led to his death. Brigham also told Porter that he and Taylor felt the mob action was comparatively insignificant to the work of the temple, even though families were being driven out, because "no lives were taken." Porter had never realized until this moment the importance placed on the temple by what he was certain were heavenly powers who directed the living oracles of the church.

That day, September 12, 1845, Brigham had received reports about further mobbing that morning. Church leaders had sent a number of wagon teams off to bring in grain from the settlements. Brigham had told them, "The object of our enemies (in burning the settlements) is to get opposition (from us) enough to raise popular excitement (from the locals), but we think it best to let them burn up our homes while we take care of our families and grain. Let the sheriff of Hancock County attend to the mob . . . "

Brigham finished his report to Porter. The two shook hands and Porter left, ready to find his partner Return Jackson Redden and head south to bring in families who had been burned out of their farms.

At that moment, in Carthage, Hancock County Sheriff Jacob Backenstos thanked a neighbor for a warning that his life was in danger. Backenstos had been targeted for assassination.

"The reason?" asked Backenstos to the same neighbor.

"For trying to recruit the folks of Carthage to protect the Mormons."

"Even though a bunch of Mormon farms were burned out last night?"

"Yep. Especially for that."

Sheriff Backenstos left Carthage and rode his buggy straight for Nauvoo. He was at that moment riding in a fast trot for two reasons — for his own safety and to raise a posse, now from among the Mormons, since no one else seemed willing to help him, in order to protect rural Mormon settlers who lived away from the safety of Nauvoo.

Backenstos was tall and stout. He had fair hair, still thick, and possessed a rough cordiality. Just recently elected, he had come to his first crossroads — of either performing his job dutifully or using it to catapult himself into the political arena where his deepest aspirations lay. Despite his better judgment, he was now helping the Mormons. As with Alexander Doniphan in Missouri, whose story of which he was somewhat aware, he was committing political suicide, he realized, but the Mormons were being treated unjustly, and that fact alone just downright angered him.

As he rode towards Nauvoo pondering his position, he heard horsehooves behind him. Fear shot through his heart and he realized these were no doubt his assassins. He broke his buggy into a gallop.

Frank Worrell was in the forefront of several horsemen who were charging after him, planning to shoot Backenstos dead and somehow lay the blame to the Mormons.

At Simpson's Creek, Porter and his riding partner Return Jackson Redden were refreshing their horses. The two were at that moment on their errand for Brigham to find the burned-out families when Porter glanced up and noticed Backenstos coming straight at him full speed.

"What's the matter!" shouted Porter, moving to the side of the road.

"Mob's after me!" yelled Backenstos, slowing his wagon beside him. He recognized Porter straight away as that "honorable friend" among Mormons and that "villainous rogue" among the Carthaginians. On any other occasion he would have avoided the notorious gunslinger, but today his heart leaped with hope.

"Boys," he yelled, "you are hereby deputized. Hold off that mob!"

"No mob's going to touch you!" smiled Porter with complete confidence.

Redden piped up, "I've got 50 rounds, and Porter here has 30."

Porter then discerned the horseman at the front of the pack . . . and in disbelief he stared. He knew this would be his long-awaited confrontation.

"Sheriff," said Porter. "Let me handle this alone." He walked 20 feet up the road from Backenstos and Redden, almost as if in a trance. He had heard in recent months of Frank Worrell bragging that he himself had applied the fatal shot to Joseph at the window sill. And it was this same Worrell who, upon last meeting Porter, had threatened to do away with him personally, laughing as he had left. Porter came to a stop in the road and snarled, "We'll see who laughs, my friend."

Frank Worrell spotted him, and halted his roan. He waved to his men to stay back, and they did so 50 yards behind him. He smiled as he muttered, "This boy is finally mine. Thank God for this glorious day."

Frank gazed at him, and for a moment time seemed to stand still. He had always exercised discretion through his life, and his last several meetings with Porter had proved no exception. But when he beheld Porter today, this minute, standing there with only two other men on the roadside in the middle of nowhere, he knew this was the moment of a lifetime. He glanced back at his men, now respectfully out of his way, and pulled out his favorite revolver. He turned his head to face Porter, and knew without a doubt he would live to see the Mormon outlaw in his grave this very day.

CHAPTER 56

Porter pulled two fifteen-shooter rifles plus three revolvers. Return Jackson Redden, his official back-up for this duel, took position at the side of the road with two pistols.

Sheriff Backenstos then commanded Frank Worrell to return to Carthage.

Worrell chuckled and rode forward, cocking his rifle and halting his horse 100 feet from Porter. Frank Worrell then took aim at Porter's chest.

"You're mine, Rockwell!" he shouted, and then he fired.

The shot missed. He fired again.

Dust splattered beside Porter.

Worrell was furious. He fired twice more.

More dust.

Finally, Worrell screamed and rode his horse directly at Porter, ready to club him. Porter watched the horse's hooves kicking up dust, and lost all concept of sound as he then saw Worrell's mouth contorting as it shouted like a charging banshee towards him. Porter closed one eye, raised his revolver and took aim directly at the man's belt buckle. He was not sure if he should, in fact, fire a fatal shot. Perhaps he should merely wound him. The press reports that would generate if he killed Worrell could rival the Boggs affair: Worrell was high-ranking and would be a serious martyr for the Carthage cause; the *Warsaw Signal* would so capitalize on it as to instigate a literal avalanche of bad press and probable mob action against their people. Then, Porter thought of Worrell's boastful tirade in front of the disbanded Nauvoo Legion in the woods and, most painful of all, the bragging of Joseph's death. He gazed into Worrell's eyes and suddenly heard him screaming, sounding like a demon out of Hades.

Worrell was galloping straight at him — just seconds away — now raising his rifle stock, coming in on Porter for the kill.

And then Porter pulled the trigger. His pistol thundered loudly. The gunpowder kicked the weapon up with a powerful jolt, and the lead ball thundered from the gun barrell. If it had possessed an eye, it would have seen a square-on trajectory as it closed in on the screaming, angry warrior on horseback, and it would have then seen the same horsemen's belt buckle increasing in size exponentially with each passing micro-second.

Worrell was hit dead center. The ball penetrated his belt buckle and he flew four feet into the air. He crashed to the dust, blood geysering from his wound, and Porter winced. Worrell grabbed the rifle off the ground beside him and took aim at Porter. Porter fired again. The ball hit Worrell in his chest, and the impact knocked the gun out of his hand. He then dropped his head back, and his eyes stared open. He writhed on the ground a moment, and fell limp.

The other four horsemen stared from up the hill.

"Which one of you wants to be next?" yelled Porter.

The four simply gazed at him.

"I suggest you uncock your weapons, then, and put 'em away. You can take that dog back where he belongs and bury him."

"He ain't dead yet," one mumbled.

"He will be," said Porter. "I got a good aim on him."

Sheriff Backenstos stared, astonished. "How'd you do that dead center in the belt buckle?"

"I'm not pleased." said Porter. "I was off half an inch."

When Thomas Sharp received word of Frank Worrell's death, he was stunned. He leaned over his desk, seeking to regain composure. He had spent many an afternoon drinking away the world's problems with Worrell.

He turned to Chauncey Higbee, the messenger with the news and one of the original conspirators.

"Everything I've written about Porter Rockwell so far," said Sharp, "is nothing . . . " He had trouble finishing the sentence. "Is *nothing* compared to what's coming." He then decided, "All right. We'll just have to see Rockwell flushed out into the open."

CHAPTER 57

Governor Thomas Ford sat at his desk in Springfield, Illinois, holding his newest copy of the *Warsaw Signal.* Smiling. He knew it was time he could finally move on the Mormon problem in Hancock County. Heretofore, with the exception of the *Expositor* matter, it was untouchable due to complicated political pressures. Since the Mormons had been driven out of Missouri they had garnered not only a sizeable voting bloc but a certain number of allies in his state, but with the unceasing pressure from area newspapers, he had lately sensed a major attitude shift toward the saints. The winds in fact had been shifting all of 1845, despite the Saints' increasing numbers. When they had settled Nauvoo they had been able to boast of 18 congregational "branches," but now had 34, due primarily to the hordes of British converts arriving from the labors of hard-working missionaries. The first "stake," like a diocese, had consisted of several branches and had been organized in Nauvoo on October 5, 1839, five months after their arrival. Consequential of their growth, six other stakes had to be established between

July and November 1840 in the outlying communities. Joseph later had dissolved these outlying stakes in order to encourage his members to move into Nauvoo to build the temple. But when not enough of their people would move, the temple's greatest ali had become violence. Ironically, these recent events in the fall of 1845 was the needed catalyst to push their people to Nauvoo for safety and in the process to begin working harder on the temple. Meanwhile, of course, these events were both painful and costly to the Mormons individually. But to Governor Ford, it was a good time to see the saints expelled altogether. The press had seasoned the state's voters very intelligently, and he had to now smile when he thought of the great manipulator, Thomas S. Sharp.

Brigham Young rode the next morning to the edge of a field. There, General J. J. Hardin waited impatiently. Brigham dismounted and faced him sternly.

"May I ask the purpose of your presence?" said Brigham.

"To find Porter Rockwell and crush the uprising," said General Hardin.

Brigham gazed across the field at the peaceful city streets and mumbled, "What uprising?"

"We have it on good authority you have an uprising," said the general.

"That sounds adventurous — I'd like to see it."

Hardin scowled at him.

"Who sent you?" said Brigham.

"The governor himself. He gave me orders to unroof every house in Nauvoo if I have to."

"Why?" said Brigham.

"To find the troublemakers."

"What troublemakers?"

The general sniffed, "Stop playing games with me. Where is Porter Rockwell?"

"What's he supposed to have done now?"

"He murdered Frank Worrell."

"You call a gunfight murder?" said Brigham.

"I wasn't there."

"That's my point. But two witnesses were, including Hancock County's own sheriff."

"In any case," said the general, "the *Signal* says Rockwell is leading a band of 300 Mormon fighters, sweeping down on innocent farmers and threatening their lives."

"That's pretty bold," said Brigham.

"It's what the governor read."

"So does the governor believe everything he reads?"

"You'd have to ask him," said Hardin.

"And you, General, what do you believe?"

Hardin cleared his throat. "Rockwell is on a rampage, and I'll secure peace in Nauvoo if I have to do it myself."

Brigham studied him a moment and muttered, "You were our closest ally." He shook his head. "He truly has gotten to you."

"I beg your pardon?"

"Sharp. Didn't your mama teach you to not believe everything you read in the newspaper?"

"I repeat . . . I have orders from Governor Ford, and —" Brigham cut in, "No need to go through that again, General. Porter Rockwell is not here. So what else do you want?"

"I am ordered to search the Mansion House stables for the bodies of two men last seen in Nauvoo, and it is supposed they are murdered."

Brigham sighed, "You're welcome to search for dead bodies or anything else."

"Do you know anything about them?" said Hardin with a glare.

Brigham met his glare:

"No, but I have reliable information that some one hundred Mormon houses have been burned in the south part of the county. Perhaps if you go there you'll find your murderers."

Hardin gazed at him curiously, and for a moment doubt crept in as to what he had been told about the saints, but he swept the thought away, spit a wad of tobacco near Brigham's boot, and stomped off.

Brigham stared at him leaving, concerned that the governor himself was getting involved. It seemed no longer a local issue, and he suspected the entire state government was gathering its forces. It was now also obvious that all their allies — as General Hardin had once so solidly been — were slowly evaporating.

CHAPTER 58

Birds warbled as twilight peacefully ushered in on Hancock County meadows.

Torches flickered and bounced from the distant eastern horizon, emerging from the darkening day with men on horseback. The last faint remnants of light gleamed in the sky.

Fifty men with torches stopped at a farmhouse.

Curiously surprised at all the commotion, Jason Call came to his door. Although he wore large spectacles he was strangely unconscious of other people. He was a devoted family man and generally kept to himself. If ever confronted he would be the first to turn his cheek. However, if his ire were raised, he could assume the demeanor of a wolverine.

Call was grabbed by the strangers, jerked away from his house, and ushered to a tree. There he was tied with his arms around it.

His wife and 15-year-old daughter saw a bowie knife stuck through the shirt on Call's back. The shirt was ripped open. The knife had not touched him.

Levi Williams rippled a 16-foot bullwhip and straddled up beside him. Williams had known Frank Worrell since childhood, and was still livid over Worrell's death. They had in their teenage years caroused and drunk together. Like Worrell, Levi believed his current activities were an act of community defense.

"We can't find Porter Rockwell," said Levi Williams, "and he's acquaintances with you, ain't he?"

Jason Call was so surprised over what was happening that he could not even think to reply.

"It looks like Porter's playing fox with us," said Williams. "But I reckon the hounds have taken all they can take; 'you understand me?"

Call said nothing.

"So where is he?"

Call glanced back at Levi Williams. A shiver passed over his face.

"Answer me."

Call's shock suddenly turned to anger. "I wouldn't tell you if I knew."

Levi Williams swore at him and walked 10 paces back. He played with the leather whip a moment, then stared at Call's back. He asked him again. "Where's Porter?"

Call said nothing.

Williams reared back slowly, then thrust the whip lash forward. The knotted leather slashed into his flesh and blood shot from a deep gash.

Call gasped and his wife screamed. Two men grabbed her and their daughter and held them.

"Your wife's watching till you talk. Now tell us where he's at."

"Any dog worth his salt," said Call, "should sniff him out on his own."

"You'll feel salt all right — we'll throw it on your back when we're finished! You get 20 lashes!" Williams whipped him again. The leather entered the first wound and cut next to the bone. Call trembled. Williams strode up next to him:

"You gonna talk, boy? Or take all 20?"

Call spat at him.

"All right, there goes your barn," said Williams.

Levi Williams nodded to a horseman holding a torch, and the horseman tossed it into the barn. As the building went up in flames, Williams glanced at Jason Call's wife. Suddenly Williams reared back and lashed again.

Call gasped.

"If you don't know where he's at, tell us who else knows Porter."

"Everybody!"

"Who else close?"

"Nobody!"

"Give me one name who'll know where he's at."

"You ain't puttin' that leather to nobody you don't need to," said Jason Call.

Williams was enraged. He reared back and lashed again.

Call collapsed and was held by the rope around the tree, his arms hanging straight, his legs limp.

The barn became an inferno. The red flames flickered off Call's red-streamed back. "My horse is in there — get him out," shouted Call.

The horse whinnied and screamed, but soon fell silent. Call pled for the animal's life. Levi Williams stood motionless.

"Let it out — he's my only horse!" said Call. "We need him for plowing!"

"You know what you gotta do," said Williams.

Call stared at the fire consuming the barn. He scowled at the faces surrounding him. He looked at Williams. "If Porter hears of this, you're dead meat."

"We'll see who's dead meat." Williams then reared back and lashed him the hardest yet.

Call shouted with pain.

"You open up, boy, or I'm gonna open you up . . . " said Williams.

Call remained silent.

Another 15 lashes came slowly, and Call meanwhile dangled and writhed, but was silent with each blow.

Williams finally turned to Call's daughter, "Tell your papa he's gonna get all 20 'lest he talks."

She was in shock and said nothing.

Williams turned and lashed again. And again. And again . . .

One of Williams' men mumbled, "I think he's left us."

"What's that?" said Williams.

"He's gone. Look at him."

Williams put down the whip and walked up to Call, who was still dangling there, now with his eyes open and staring off, white as a sheet.

"You're right," said Williams. "Cut him down."

Call's wife and daughter screamed and ran to him. They caught him as he was cut from the tree, and held his lifeless body.

And cried.

CHAPTER 59

At Jason Call's funeral forty souls gathered in the blistering heat. Porter and a dozen others were among the last to arrive. The meadow was green and hazy. Songbirds chittered as the sun filtered through thin clouds.

Most of the people at the funeral knew why Call was dead. But Porter had been in the woods of southern Hancock County for two days and was just now joining the funeral procession with Emily, from whom he had only an hour earlier learned of the funeral.

As the opening hymn began, Porter and Emily approached the gathering. His long hair was braided in a pony tail down his back, covered by a high collar.

Several minutes into the eulogy, he overheard news that astonished him. Someone whispered, "Is that who Brother Call was killed over?"

"What do you mean?" spoke up Porter.

Several people turned to him for the disruption.

The man beside him said quietly, "Call wouldn't tell the mob where you were at — so they killed him."

Porter was dumbstruck. He gaped at Call's widow across the gathering, and felt indescribable anguish. Then, from over the hill, he heard the thundering of horsehooves. The sermon suddenly stopped. Porter gazed atop the vale surrounding the meadow and saw a hundred horsemen appearing, led by Levi Williams.

All forty members of the funeral service stared in disbelief. Porter was the first to verbally shake the silent air:

"To the woods!"

That single sentence broke the crowd from its trance. Some ran to their horses. Others scrambled to the forest. He shouted to Emily to stay with him and they took out running for the trees.

Only two Mormons had weapons in their saddlebags. But as they ran to grab them, their guns were shot away. They now had nowhere to escape but the forest.

As Emily ran beside Porter they neared the woods.

The Illinois horsemen put away their guns, then came thundering down the hill . . . pulling out bullwhips.

They swarmed on the funeral party like cattle.

Porter turned and saw Levi Williams lash his whip at the ankles of the first man he came upon, tripping him into the earth. Then a dozen others were whipped across their backs and faces while running.

Several of the funeral party escaped on horseback, but most of even those were lashed repeatedly before they rode out of the vale.

The others on foot panicked and continued stampeding for the forest.

Porter and Emily made it to the cover of trees. A horseman approached them but they hid against a thick oak. The horseman rode slowly past, as Porter and Emily backed around the other side of the tree, and the man never saw them and rode away.

Then another horseman rode through thick brush and spotted them. As he reared back his bullwhip, Porter knew he would move mountains before he'd let anyone harm his precious daughter. He did not even have to make a choice: He leapt onto the horse, grabbed the rider, and toppled him to the ground. There, Porter reached for his knife — but the man caught his wrist. Porter was stronger however and moved it slowly toward the man's chest.

Suddenly, he heard a gun cocked. He glanced up and saw Levi Williams aiming directly at him. He dove to the side and Williams fired.

CHAPTER 60

Levi Williams' shot struck a tree. His horse panicked and reared. Levi struggled to turn the horse, but Porter jumped up and grabbed him. Both men fell to the ground.

Porter backhanded him. Williams fell back against a tree, dazed.

Emily meanwhile saw a whip on the ground and grabbed it. She reared back to lash Levi Williams, whose ankle was turned. Williams was unable to stand. He swore at her, drunk with anger, and she lashed him anyway. Now, he was beside himself with fury and began crawling towards her. She lashed again and he screeched with frustration and pain. Porter caught sight of it and laughed. Levi glared at them both and wiped the blood from his cheek.

Porter grabbed Emily and hugged her. Williams threatened to kill them.

"You're welcome to, mister," said Porter, "if you can crawl as fast as we can ride."

Porter and Emily mounted Levi Williams' horse and took off in a bold gallop. Porter had no idea William had been responsible for killing Jason Call or he likely would have stayed around to accomplish other business.

Meanwhile, the Carthage horsemen searched for others in the woods.

Porter breathed heavily with concern for his daughter as they rode. In the distance he heard the horsemen cheering, finishing their attack on the funeral and riding away.

He and Emily came to a clearing. They could see a half dozen cabins burning, and could also see two groups of other horsemen — now with torches — rendezvousing on a distant country road.

Without a word to Emily of where he was riding, Porter led the horse into thicker woods.

Emily held on behind for twenty minutes and neither spoke. Finally she broke the silence.

"Where're we going?"

He didn't answer. Because of his peculiar intensity, she felt it best to remain silent.

When they arrived at his woodland cabin, they found it in ashes. Under a loose brick in the chimney he pulled out a pistol. He heard whining, and strode around the cabin's remains. He found his dog on the ground, bleeding from a bullet wound. Emily ran to it, crying. Porter pulled her away. "Ugly must've heard all the commotion out here in the woods, all the way from my ma's," said Porter. "That's where he's been staying, but he musta' been worried about me and came to check up on me."

"He's a faithful friend," isn't he?" said Emily.

He knelt beside Ugly and patted his forehead. He stood and stared at it a moment, then pulled out his pistol. He cocked it and Emily turned her head.

"Papa," she said, "please don't."

Porter could not fire. He recalled the years he had spent with the animal, and for a moment he saw it as a puppy. Fully fifteen seconds passed before he put the gun to the dog's head. Another ten seconds passed. Finally Emily heard the hammer uncocked.

Porter turned his head. Emily saw his eyes moist. He knew he could not kill Ugly if there was a decent chance he could live — and without pain for very long. He went to his medicine pouch, removed healing herbs, and applied them to Ugly's wound.

"At lest the lead ball went out the other side," said Porter, "and with any luck, maybe it missed his vital organs. Some of these plants will kill the pain for him while he heals."

"Will he live?" said Emily.

"The Lord willing."

"Do dogs go to heaven, Pa?"

"Joseph taught they have souls, so yeah, depending on where we go, we'll see our loved ones again — including our animals we loved."

"Will they be able to talk to us?" she said.

"Joseph taught they'll be at our judgement and testify if we was mean or good to them."

"Well, Ugly will have a lot of good things to say about you, huh, Papa? You've been really good to him."

Porter smiled and stroked Ugly's large head.

Soon they again heard horses galloping. He grabbed her arm and dashed to the cover of trees.

"What about Ugly?" she cried.

"He'll be all right till we get back. He'll either die soon or live. Them herbs are fast-healing."

At his neighbors' barn, Porter saddled up a second horse for Emily.

Within minutes, as they rode, he glanced back and noticed they were being pursued. He nodded to Emily to follow him, and they broke into a gallop.

CHAPTER 61

Ahead was a road-crossing. Down one lane Porter and Emily could see a dozen riders approaching. On the other were two dozen. Porter glanced back and saw they were still being followed by the first group and that they were now caught between the three on-coming parties. He glanced both directions at the crossroads and saw the forces coming closer, about to hem them in. Then he noticed the riders raising their rifles. He finally gazed at Emily and she read his look.

They were trapped.

But far from captured.

Porter studied the fence to their side. He gave her a nod and they spurred their horses. They galloped 30 yards and leaped the fence.

Their pursuers broke into a gallop and rode around both ends of the fence.

This gave Porter and Emily additional seconds to gain distance on their enemy. And they soon came to a river. They splashed into it and swam their horses to the other side.

When their pursuers arrived at the shore, they discovered horseshoe prints in the mud, and decided to cross. They were unaware that Porter and Emily had already, upstream, circled back and re-crossed the river . . .

Under a starlit sky Emily sat beside Porter at the water's edge.

"I bet Mama's worried," she said.

Porter glanced at her curiously. "I reckon she's more than worried; she's prob'ly half dead with concern."

"Sure wish things were different."

"How do you feel about Alpheas?" he said.

"He's all right, I reckon."

"You reckon?"

"The young ones talk to him and like him, but then they don't know you — not like I do."

Porter took that as the greatest compliment he'd ever heard. Her love was keeping him sane, he figured. Under the moonlight that night Emily fell asleep with her head on her pa's lap. Porter pulled a saddle blanket over the rest of her, exposing his own legs to the chilly air, and he stared at the starlight on the stream, finally drifting asleep.

Dawn diffused its softening glow on the forest, and Porter arose. Emily was already at the river, washing her morning face. He knelt beside her. He studied her kind demeanor, her devotion to him, and noted the incredible contrast between her and Luana, but said nothing.

They rode their horses an hour before discovering a band of horsemen. Suddenly to their side, a gunshot sounded. In panic, Emily's horse ran. A flurry of shots followed and branches shattered about her head.

Porter tried to follow but Emily and her horse disappeared in thick underbrush. He wondered if she were hit. As he searched for her, the horsemen did not pursue him. He wondered if they had found her. So he circled back. There were no traces of her. The idea of losing Emily churned his insides with a pain stronger than he had ever experienced.

He scoured the woods, but found nothing.

He came to a large meadow. As he began riding across it he felt unusually vulnerable. He scanned the forest on both sides and felt increasing uneasiness. He heard strange bird calls to his right. He shot a look there. Nothing. He wondered if he would ever find Emily.

As he approached the center of the meadow, he sensed his danger heightening, but also felt no alternative than to continue across the unprotected clearing. The protection of the forest was just ahead.

Arriving at the edge of the woods, he discovered a man lying in tall grass, holding his thigh and groaning.

"Can you help me, mister?"

"What's the matter?" said Porter.

"I was thrown."

When Porter knelt to look him over, the man rolled to his side, pulled out a pistol, and pointed it straight at Porter's neck.

Six more men jumped him from behind — and all held their rifles aimed.

CHAPTER 62

At a campfire Porter sat with his hands tied. The evening was cool and he shivered. A guard sat across the fire from him, gazing into the thicket. Fifty yards away through thick trees, a hundred mob members held torches and cheered their speaker. Porter was not surprised to descry through the foliage Levi Williams near the speaker, but he was somewhat taken back to discover the speaker himself was Thomas Sharp. He scanned the area and realized Emily was not their prisoner. He wondered if she were still alive.

Levi was livid. He was still sore from Porter's humiliating him and was determined to exact his revenge. He left the mob, tromped through the brush, stridled up to Porter and backhanded him. Porter took the blow and merely glared at him.

"You'll see what happens to those who resist righteous forces," muttered Levi.

Porter smirked at him, thinking him an idiot.

Through the thicket a hangman's noose was dropped over a tree. His own horse was untied and brought to him by two young men. Porter would be placed on it with the noose around him and the horse would be smacked, leaving him dangling.

He could hear the mob, most of whom were half-drunk, now shouting for his death. He glanced across the fire at his horse and finally muttered to himself.

"Enough of this."

He jumped up, leaped over the fire, and smashed his head into Levi's abdomen. Simultaneously, his fingers grasped the knife in Levi's belt. With his hands still tied he clasped the handle and in a flash sliced the knots loose.

He ran straight for his horse and jerked the reins from its wrangler. He jumped on it and launched a gallop into the woods.

The men pulled pistols and fired — but the shots only cracked branches beside him — and he sped away, leaving the mob screaming at him. Several mounted their horses and began pursuit.

Thomas Sharp ran to the clearing and beheld Porter disappearing. The war was over anyway, he mused, and he had decisively won. His paper was a booming success now and the Mormon movement would trail into the desert and die, much like a comet that flashes in the night and trails into oblivion. He smiled at his victory, and yet that could not preclude a faint smile of involuntary admiration for the wily, notorious gunslinger, who always got away.

Sharp rode back to Warsaw, planning a final printed epitaph to Brigham Young, who — unknown to the Mormons —

was about to be arrested by a U.S. marshal and locked away, only to be mobbed and killed like Joseph. "I'll have the last laugh," smiled Sharp. As for Porter, he had come up with something to print about him, too. It had turned into a game for him, to see how many lives this wildcat actually had.

Brigham's followers would in Sharp's mind have to move to an untamed territory, perhaps north to Canada or west to Iowa or south to Texas, and there be butchered by Indians or ravaged by disease and starvation, with their entire civilization vanishing within five years. Four years at best. Give it three. Of this he felt such a certainty that he would ride to his office immediately and proclaim a front page declaration of the fact. Merely seeing Brigham arrested would give him immense satisfaction. He had grown over these few years from amused detachment of the saints to dissatisfaction and even anger at their power and doctrine, and finally to establishing them in his mind as some sort of opponents in a chess game. He now received monumental enjoyment at seeing them defeated, just as he would any worthy opponent in a good game. He smiled all the way to the office.

Several dozen mobbers were soon on horseback giving chase, but Porter was miles ahead. He could see their torches shimmering behind him in the distance, and they soon disappeared. If only he could find Emily.

Then he heard a whistle. He turned and . . . there she was, hiding at a river bank!

In order to evade her pursuers she had jumped from her horse into the cover of a deep thicket, then had rolled all the way through it onto a sloshy, muddy riverbank. Her pursuers had followed her horse all the way to the outskirts of Nauvoo, where they had given up.

Relieved to the point of tears, he hugged her and helped her mount his horse. She was covered head to foot with loose, slimy mud. Only her bright blue eyes sparking in the moonlight gave any indication the creature was his daughter. They arrived in Nauvoo at midnight, where Emily's horse was waiting at the outskirts of town.

They rode to Luana's cabin. Luana greeted them, saw Emily drenched in mud, and broke out complaining. She immediately demanded to know what she had been doing and why she was home so late.

"Just another day with Papa," quipped Emily. She never would tell Luana her day's experience, and certainly Porter never would. Luana would forever assume her daughter had spent a quiet day at a funeral . . .

Emily went to sleep that night smiling.

CHAPTER 63

Porter immediately went back to his woodland cabin to find Ugly.

He rode through eastern city farmlands to find his beloved animal, figuring him to be more than likely dead by now. He was prepared to bury his old friend. He knew the herbs had taken the pain away until he could return to see if it were either dead or if the healing process had begun.

As he arrived at his concealed woodland hideout, he was surprised to find Ugly walking slowly to him, tail wagging.

"Well, you're back to your old self, fella," said Porter cheerily. "I can see you've rolled in something awful strong."

Ugly barked.

"Not so loud, boy. Enemy are still all around." He grabbed a soap bar from his small storage shed that was left unburned, and he washed Ugly in the nearby creek. "Fortunately, this is easy going. You've only got some smushed dead critter on one part of your back. So this'll only take a minute. Count your lucky stars, boy, 'cause if you'd rolled this thing all over you, I think I'd be putting a lead ball in your head right now just to put you out of my misery." He smiled and Ugly wagged his tail harder, happy to see his old master. Porter suddenly remembered his daughter's concern. "Won't Emily be glad to see you!" His daughter had never worried, he realized, and it was actually her faith that likely had helped the dog to heal.

When he finished cleaning Ugly's back, he rigged up the animal onto his horse to ride behind him on part of the saddle, tying him so he wouldn't fall off since he still was weak from the wound. "This thing healed real fast, boy. 'Guess this was only a flesh wound after all, and nothing got infected. I better bring this bag of herbs and this soap bar along as well, huh? I got a feeling we're gonna need one of these over the years — and I would guess it's the soap — wouldn't you say?"

Ugly wagged his tail and off they rode. Porter heard horsemen about, but he kept off the road and traveled slowly in the woods nearby so as not to be seen.

He arrived with Ugly at the safety of the city's center and rode down Parley's Street to Luana's. Emily was the first to see them coming. She ran out to greet them, and cried — while she laughed — at seeing Ugly rigged up with ropes on the horse, with all four legs holding onto Porter for dear life.

"I think Ugly has this down," said Porter. "When he gets stronger, I do believe he'll be able to ride without the ropes."

"Do you two plan on traipsing about the countryside like this together?" said Luana with a smile, coming outside with the other kids, who quickly created a commotion. Emily had told them all of Ugly being shot, but had reassured them he would be all right. in any case they were all joyous to see him with their father.

"Well if he gets tired of walking or gets too old to," said Porter, "I reckon he could ride with me all he wants."

"I wish someone took care of *me* like that," smiled Luana.

"Every time I offer you to ride with me, honey," said Porter, "you cut the ropes!"

She chuckled at his accurate analysis. She knew deep down she had always pushed him away emotionally — even when he did give her attention — but she brushed the thought away, not wanting to admit it. "You kids visit with Ugly a few minutes, then your pa is taking him back to his ma's."

"I reckon so," grumbled Porter. "We don't want another creature in the cabin getting more love and attention than us, huh?"

Luana again knew he was right, but said nothing. The stated reason Ugly had been sent to live with Porter's mother in the first place was because they could not afford to feed him, but the unstated, deeper purpose behind the decision, which now dawned on Porter, was that the pet simply drew too much attention from the children to make Luana feel all that secure.

"You kids can go visit Ugly at your grandma's later tonight," said Luana.

Porter smiled that he was finally figuring Luana out after all these years. Even if he had known these quirks about her years earlier, it probably would not have helped the marriage anyway, he mused. He just did not know how to deal with her.

Porter took Ugly to Sarah's cabin. There, his mother, brothers, and sisters lauded over the dog. They took him down from the horse, carried him inside, and applied more herbs to him.

"I think he'll be all right," said Porter. "It's not everyone in this county who's so lucky as to get drenched with this kinda love."

"It's not everyone in this county," said his mother, "who doesn't talk back. Maybe that's what makes him so darn likeable."

"Maybe so," chuckled Porter.

Porter wished he had been clever enough to say that to Luana. But he realized his own mistakes in their marriage, so he wouldn't have said anything smart-mouthed to her even if he had thought of it, he decided.

He quickly remounted and rode off to see Brigham to learn what was needed of him. It was obvious their community was in danger, but when he arrived at Brigham's office minutes later he was surprised to learn the extent: Brigham himself was in hiding and Nauvoo, their bastian, was under siege! He already knew the rural saints were in danger, but it was news to him the city itself was now in imminent peril.

"Where is Brigham?" Porter demanded.

Hiram Kimball, a rugged, swarthy but reliable recent Mormon convert who owned Nauvoo's first store — even back when the town was "Commerce" — smirked at Porter.

"I've got orders to tell no one." He was proud he could guard both the office and the information on Brigham's whereabouts.

Porter was enraged. "You've got three reasons to tell me."

Hiram looked at him curiously. "Like what?"

Porter muttered, "The first one's this." He suddenly smashed his fist into Hiram's face, and Kimball crashed against

432

the wall, then slunk to the floor. Unexpectedly, Kimball grabbed Porter's leg and tripped him, then punched him in the stomach.

With both men on the floor Porter yelled, "Here's the second reason." He whacked him in the other cheek with his fist and Hiram fell flat on his back, dazed.

As Porter stood and staggered forward to hit him again, Hiram awkwardly arose and faced him. Both men smiled at each other. Porter found the fellow somewhat charming, as Hiram teased him to come forward. So he did. Hiram kicked him, and Porter flew backward and crashed out the window.

CHAPTER 64

Hiram painfully made his way out the door — only to be surprised by Porter waiting for him behind the door. Porter blind-sided him with a fist to his nose — shouting, "There's your third reason."

Hiram Kimball went completely cold. Moments later he awakened with a gasp as Porter threw cold water in his face. Porter grabbed his shirt and pulled him forward.

"I'll think of some more reasons for you to tell me if you need 'em."

"No, three reasons are enough," said Hiram, then he pointed to the temple on the hill. "Brigham's hiding up there in the lobby."

Porter let him go and Hiram's head thudded to the ground with a groan.

"How come you wouldn't tell me, Hiram? We're better friends than that."

"I was bored."

To the temple he galloped. Located 70 feet above much of the city, it was an imposing and inspiring sight to the Mormons and to Porter now as well as he pushed his horse on the ride up Mulholland. The structure, of pine from Wisconsin and local gray limestone, was nearly finished, and during this autumn season of 1845 Brigham had directed a concentrated effort to complete it. Three seasons earlier on January 24, 1845 Brigham had prayed with two assistants to ask God whether they should stay and finish the temple. "The answer," Brigham reported, "was we should."

Inside, Porter found Brigham conferring with aides in the foyer. Each greeted Porter joyously and shook his hand.

"We've had a dozen reports from the Illinoisans," said Brigham, "that you were trapped and killed."

"I probably was," said Porter.

The men smiled, yet Brigham remained sober. "Sheriff Backenstos was acquitted for the death of Frank Worrell, but charges are still on you."

"Brother Brigham," came Almon Babbitt's voice, booming with anger as he suddenly entered the foyer. "John Sikes, the federal marshal, is outside waiting to arrest you."

Porter watched curiously.

"On what charges?" said Brigham.

"Passing bogus money," said Babbitt.

"Preposterous." Brigham thought a moment and spoke. "All right, we'll give them their money's worth." He then sent his secretary outside who announced, "Mr. Young will be leaving the building." Then William Miller walked outside wearing Brigham's famous cap and cloak.

There, U.S. Marshal John Sikes arrested William Miller, who did in fact look strikingly similar to Brigham, even without the disguise.

Miller assured the marshal — with complete honesty in his voice — that there was some mistake, but the marshal became even more adamant: He claimed other Mormons had given him the dodge before, but this time he had his man for sure, and then he dragged Miller off to Carthage.

However, Miller demanded to perform certain errands around the city first, on his way to jail, if he was expected to cooperate with providing information they wished of him. The marshal smiled and complied. After a couple hours of this wild-goose-chase, however, the marshal grew impatient and snapped his reigns for Carthage. It was Miller's turn to smile.

In the crowded lobby of the Hamilton House the marshal learned from the barkeep that William Miller was not Brigham Young. The marshal immediately sent for two other witnesses, who strode in, stared at the fake Brigham Young, and glared at the marshal. The marshal's face turned bright red. He swore and threw a chair across the room. Others in the lobby, including Levi Williams, stomped away, furious.

William Miller, the prisoner, was promptly released when his attorney appeared. Despite his release he remained at the Hamilton House, deciding to spend the night in an upstairs room for travelers in order to avoid a potential ambush on the dark journey back home. Downstairs, meanwhile, the crowd was entertained by the story. Despite the fact they did indeed want Brigham captured, they burst into laughter over and over when they re-told the story of the marshal's mistake. William Miller could not sleep that night. His attorney — Edmunds — lay in bed in another room above the tavern, inadvertently awakening Miller and all the other sleeping travelers that night with his intermittent roars of laughter.

(Author's note: Every detail of this unusual account is historically documented.)

CHAPTER 65

When William Miller returned to Brigham the next morning, he couldn't wait to report the details.

Brigham smiled at the story, then became sober and turned to Porter. As he walked across the temple lawn with him, overlooking the city flats below, he stopped for a moment and gazed at its orchards, fields and farms, its 500 brick homes and stores, its 300 frame houses, and its 1200 log homes and wide streets, feeling a pride that the most beautiful city perhaps in America, certainly the most architecturally advanced per capita, had been built from a swamp by their industriousness. And through that pride he announced to Porter the most surprising yet long-awaited news yet.

They would leave it all behind. Their people would be going West, he told Porter, travelling across prairie and mountain to the Great Basin on the other side of the Rockies. There, they would find a land of peace and safety far from their detractors and enemies. He then prophesied "in the name of the Lord, our people will multiply in faith and numbers, and the desert will blossom as the rose."

Brigham then appointed Porter as his bodyguard. And he requested that he stay at his home from that day until the exodus.

The night previously, Porter had stayed at his mother's home, in "Ugly's room." Porter was not surprised he did not have a room so designated for himself. "But my dog does," he smiled. "Ugly, will you be gracious enough to let me stay in *your* room tonight?" he had said.

Ugly had been gracious, and let him.

There was tremendous work involved preparatory to a mass migration, including but not limited to building thousands of wagons and handcarts and the disposal of property. On September 24, 1845 the Twelve Apostles met and drafted a statement of their intention to leave.

Next they met with a state commission and presented their statement, agreeing to leave the next spring. They used the meeting for two purposes — to buy time so the mobs would back off their attacks against them and to sell their property for a price — any price — so they would not have to completely surrender it with no remuneration whatever as had occurred at Far West, Missouri in 1838, Clay County in 1836, and Jackson County three years earlier.

In order to increase sales of their property — so they could afford wagons if nothing else — the Nauvoo stake high council would publish a flier and send it to area newspapers on January 20, 1846, re-affirming to the public their commitment to actually leave and to create interest in their properties.

Still, the rabble resumed its harassment unabated — a certain number found themselves actually enjoying persecuting the Saints, and they especially wished to keep up the pressure so the Mormons really would get out.

Later that night after Brigham had announced the exodus to him, Porter strolled by the river and gazed at the moon. He wondered if Emily should travel West with him in the advance party or go later with the next wagon train. There were certain dangers itinerant to an advance party, and he was torn over what to do with her.

As he lay in his bed he could not sleep. He thought about her and the emptiness in his life. He was haunted by the last expression of love and hope he had seen in her — while she was covered in mud. He smiled at her image in his mind. He finally drifted asleep, realizing he loved her more than Luana, more than his friends and all his living family, and even more than life itself.

CHAPTER 66

In his study the next day Brigham confronted Porter with news he thought would shatter his dreams.

"Luana is getting sealed to Alpheas Cutler tomorrow."

"Good."

Brigham was baffled as Porter walked past him, whistling.

"Good?" said Brigham to himself as he stared at the closed door.

From inside Porter's room, Brigham heard his friend mutter aloud, "Poor devil," referring to Cutler, and then chuckle.

But that night at dinner, Porter learned details that cut away his appetite.

"The children will also be sealed to him," added Brigham.

Porter retired to his room and wept. Later, unable to sleep, he went to see Brigham in his study.

Brigham sat silently while Porter collected his thoughts. "I knew of the wedding — that it would be soon — and I learned to live with it. But the sealing of the children away from me — I guess I never thought that would be this soon," said Porter.

"The children will choose who they wish as their father in the next life," explained Brigham. "So it won't matter anyway who the actual sealing is to now, will it?"

Brigham inspected his face a few seconds and felt increasing compassion. "Pray over it, Porter, that's what the Spirit, the Comforter, is for; you know that."

Porter said nothing but retired to his room again and sat. Where would Emily fit into the picture? He would study the stars all night. Outside he took a walk.

He was still walking the next morning when Luana and Cutler appeared with the four children at the temple entrance.

It was 11 A.M. when Porter hid in the shadows of the nearest building. His eyes went from each of his kids to the memory of each of their births . . .

He was still standing, staring at the temple door, when the new family of six emerged an hour later. They seemed ebullient. He saw Luana place her arms around Cutler's neck and kiss him affectionately.

Porter turned his head. He strolled behind the building and down another street. He found himself staring at the tavern door. He thought a moment, then glanced upstreet at the temple again. He beheld his family standing with Cutler, in one final glimpse, and he looked in the tavern again. He decided getting drunk was not the right answer to his trials, so he simply returned to Brigham's house.

From his bedroom Brigham heard him clomp up the stairs.

Porter pulled off his boots and lay on his bed. For the second night in a row he didn't sleep, and simply gazed out the window at the moon.

CHAPTER 67

Within days the mobs swarmed the countryside like hornets. In freezing mid-winter temperatures Brigham's people began crossing the Mississippi. The first to line up for the exodus was Charles Shumway who arrived at the Nauvoo Ferry Crossing with his ox-drawn wagon at dawn on February 4, 1846. At the foot of Parley Street he wanted to be the first to cross.

A flat-bottomed boat, propelled by a paddle wheel, approached him in zero degree weather. For several years the ferryboats had been owned by the church, and their operators would now work exhaustingly to ferry one wagon at a time — by the thousands — across the river to Montrose, Iowa.

For a short period, the Mississippi would freeze over, allowing wagons to cross the iced-over river.

When the ice melted again, the ferries would be back in full shifts.

Mob activity increased, and cannon were called in from neighboring counties. One mobber was so bold as to board a ferryboat, then halfway into the river turn to look at a

Mormon and his two sons, smile, and spit tobacco juice into the eyes of an ox. It plunged into the river, dragging another ox with it and tearing off one of the sideboards. This caused the water to flow into the flatboat. Approaching the Iowa shore the boat sank. All the boat's inhabitants, cold and exhausted, were picked up by other ferries, but the oxen drowned. Some belongings floated away and were never recovered. Had Porter been aboard, some speculated, the mobber would have joined those items to have floated away and never been recovered . . .

Upon arriving in Iowa, hundreds of Saints settled at Sugar Creek, six miles west of Montrose, for several weeks while others forged on with Brigham's advance company all the way to Winter Quarters, Nebraska. There in Nebraska, Brigham quickly established temporary church headquarters. Along the way, hundreds of wagons stopped to make winter camp in various spots.

At the first staging ground at Sugar Creek, Iowa across the Mississippi River from Nauvoo, about 800 Saints were camped by late February, 1846, many of them with less than two weeks provisions. Adding to their travail were unrelenting snowstorms. Most people gathered in makeshift shelters waiting for spring before resuming the journey westward.

Two of Porter's acquaintances improvised shelter typical of most: Lorenzo Snow arrived February 6, 1846 at Sugar Creek where he sewed two wagon covers together to make a tent since they had fled "in much haste," he later reported; Hosea Stout meanwhile prepared for his first night by making a tent out of bed clothes. His wife could hardly sit up and his little son was so sick with high fever that he noticed practically nothing around him. When the snowstorms hit, hundreds became ill from exposure. Dozens died.

Back at the river, Porter helped families load their wagons onto ferryboats. He looked up and noticed on the eastern shore, just south of the city, the mob's cannon arriving and being set into place. Their intention was to terrorize the last saints as they arrived across the river.

Porter raced his horse to his family. He helped them load their most prized belongings in a wagon, while Cutler remained silent. Luana discerned Porter's different attitude — accepting the new marriage — and she noticed he hardly paid her any attention. He was focused on his four children, and especially, as usual, Emily. Porter had learned recently that the mobs would allow those who disavowed the faith to stay. He felt grateful Luana and Cutler were strong enough in their convictions to move away from their property and make the trek. Some fifteen hundred of their 12,000 people chose to remain in Nauvoo, plus perhaps 700 more who could only later make the trip, due to lack of funds.

Porter was then very surprised when Luana and Alpheas agreed to his request:

"I wanna take Emily with me."

"Where?"

"Where we're going — across the river — and across Iowa to the new camp."

"You can have her a couple weeks," said Luana. "Then you must return her to us. But don't cross into Nebraska — we won't get that far."

Porter was thrilled to have her again. He saddled up her traveling supplies and they rode at a fast pace through all the confusion:

Porter stopped at his mother's home at the north end of town. His brothers and sisters had packed her belongings, loaded the wagon, and were now heading off to the barge.

Porter yelled, "You forgot somebody!" He ran inside and found Ugly rolling on a deceased rat in the attic. "Now is not the time to be doing that! Not when you're in close quarters with human folk. Now stop that and get out to the wagon!"

Ugly paused a moment, looked at him as if to say, "Hold your horses, human," then resumed rolling on the rat, his gigantic tail wagging at his extreme enjoyment and perhaps, Porter surmised, at his own humor. This, Ugly had learned long ago, was his supreme method of teasing Porter.

Porter yelled again.

The tail wagged harder.

Outside, the Rockwell family wagon rolled down Main Street, turned left onto Parley Street, and drove towards the barge. Porter sat beside Ugly, not wanting him in the street amidst hundreds of other wagon wheels that could roll over him.

Porter's daughter, mother, brothers, and sisters groaned amidst chuckles at Ugly's odor.

A hundred of these late-leaving families in wagons were now rolling to the river to board a barge. Suddenly they heard explosions. Ahead they could see people on barges ducking cannon shot, and others across the river racing from where the barges disembarked to the safety of the woods. Cannon balls exploded near the wagons across the river, and their horses galloped for the forest.

Porter noticed the Neff family (John, Mary, and Mary Ann — the girl he'd saved in the woods from the mob) fifty yards back, unable to control their horses and therefore unable to hitch them to their wagon. The explosions were causing the horses to panic. Porter told his brothers, sisters and mother to keep going toward the barge and to cross the river. He and Emily then jumped off the wagon and ran back to the Neff's. He grabbed the reigns, soothed the horses as well as possible amidst the thundering noises, and hitched them to the wagon. Emily watched proudly as her father saved the family of three from likely having to leave their wagon and walk West.

She and Porter helped the Neffs load their wagon. Then they ran through the streets to catch up with his mother, brothers and sisters, whose wagon — and the Neffs — were the last two to board the barge. Porter and Emily jumped aboard just as the barge gait was shut, and re-joined their family. Ugly barked, enjoying all the excitement.

As they made their way across the Mississippi, Porter glanced back and noticed a hundred roughnecks now loading their cannons and jeering, drinking and laughing. He glanced at his family, grateful he could be with and protect them. He only wished his other three children besides Emily — and that Luana — were with him, so he could oversee their safety. He shook his head at the amazing sight of enemy firing canon at them. He felt a heartache seeing it, and knowing he was leaving Joseph buried behind. He could not help but blame himself about Joseph, despite his orders to stay out of the way. *If only he and Redden had acted faster.* Cannon balls exploded while others landed in the nearby water. Emily began to cry, and Porter held her in his arms where she calmed down.

When they arrived across the river onto the Iowa shore, Porter and Emily helped his family and the Neffs run off the barge. Porter was leading the horses, running with them and holding their reigns, racing toward the safety of the woods. Emily meanwhile held onto his belt and ran faster than she ever had in her life.

Across the river, five new canon arrived — with longer range barrels — and were cranked up by the mob to fire at the last escaping refugees.

CHAPTER 68

As the last saints sped toward the woods, more cannon balls exploded — those from the new, longer-range artillery. Children around them cried. Porter spotted one small boy alone, separated from his parents who had been on the last barge with Porter. He picked him up and ran to the safety of the woods.

A whole new bombardment of cannon balls came — landing near the several dozen people running to the woods. Porter glanced to the side and saw his family running near him — his mother and sisters and brothers running alongside and pushing the wagon. Emily ran out of breath, so, while still running, Porter reached down, picked her up with his free arm, and now ran with *two* children towards the safety of the woods.

Beside him a cannon ball exploded. Its impact knocked him over. Both children landed safely in the dirt. Porter picked them up again and resumed running. He glanced to both sides and noticed other families running amidst other cannon explosions.

They finally arrived at the woods, out of artillery range. And the cannon fire ceased. The parents of the lad whom Porter held thanked him and took their son. Porter glimpsed back and noticed Brigham and the rest at the cover of trees ahead. No more of their people were exposed to the cannon, so Porter felt relieved. Then he gazed across the river at the mob jeering, shouting and laughing. As Emily grabbed his waist and hugged him, he observed — far across the river — looters on the city's main streets crashing into businesses and stealing goods by the hundreds. He felt anger as he'd rarely felt. And complete hopelessness. He saw and heard additional throngs laughing and looting and running up Parley Street in cheers. All their hard work and industriousness — and all their property — for what it was vainly worth, he realized — had come down to this.

He turned away from the scene and began his trek with Emily across Iowa.

During their journey to the western end of the state, he and Emily aided their people night and day. His daughter sought to be as helpful as her pa, and for that he was proud.

On their trek, he walked beside his mother's wagon, and finally had time to ponder the recent events. He felt remorse leaving not only Joseph behind but the small secret garden and the city's magnificent buildings he had helped construct, especially his mother's beautiful house, and their temple. Again, he pondered, they were only material possessions.

His family would be safe in this new land, and that's all that mattered. As they retired to their tent in Iowa each night, Emily would re-cap to her father the day's events of travelling and helping others, often laughing, occasionally crying, but always thrilled to be with a father who cared about every word she said.

They arrived at Council Bluffs at the far western end of the Iowa territory. This was a headquartering camp, similar to the next one they'd have at Winter Quarters, Nebraska. As Porter and Emily walked through camp they found people constructing dozens more wagons to make the journey to the Rocky Mountains. Porter was grateful his mother, brothers and sisters were all safe. They were proud to see Emily adore her father so much, and they laughed and joked with her. As always, Porter's mother was especially fond of her. But despite the celebration and the feeling of hope in the air of finding a desert home and making it an oasis, free of all prejudiced mobs, Porter was anxious to find his other three children — and also Luana.

CHAPTER 69

The next morning Brigham approached Porter at a campfire with his usual, "Good morning," then, with no prefacing small talk, gave him an unexpected assignment.

"I want you to return to Nauvoo with letters for our people who are still there."

He prepared their travel gear and announced to Emily he was returning her to her ma earlier than expected.

"But I want to go with you!" insisted Emily.

"I do, too — but you can't. 'Too dangerous back there."

Emily argued but to no avail. They searched for and arrived at Luana's and Alpheas' camp before sundown. Porter hugged each of his children, feeling their increasing coolness to him, precipitated by their mother's comments about him, he figured. And then he hugged Emily goodbye and headed directly eastward.

Emily watched him disappear in the twilight, wishing more than all she had to give that she could be with him.

After his mail trip to Nauvoo, Porter returned to Council Bluffs, and within the next two months, from March 14 to May 8, 1846, he made four more trips to Nauvoo, acting as Brigham's chief messenger.

On the eve of his final journey he met with Brigham.

"Take this letter to Almon Babbitt. He's wrapping up our final business in the city. Porter, whatever you do, stay out of trouble and just deliver the letter to him and get out."

Porter felt like punching the traitor, Babbitt, but knew Brigham was finding his services significantly important, and therefore decided he would hold his tongue — and his fists — until another day and merely obey Brigham's wishes.

It was evening when he arrived at Nauvoo for his final trip. The moon cast an eerie glow on the nearly-deserted, once-teeming city. He found Almon Babbitt at the Mulholland Street address Brigham had told him, and delivered the letter.

"So, said Babbitt," we meet again."

"So we do," said Porter through gritted teeth.

"Someday we'll have to talk," said Babbitt cheerily, "and clear the air."

Porter slowly shook his head at the pathetic soul. "Yeah, someday we'll have to clear up everything."

A mist quickly clouded the air, so thick in fact he could see no more than 30 feet. Porter wanted to leave Nauvoo immediately, recalling Brigham's recent advice, so he rode directly west to go downhill towards the ferry. While still on Mulholland Street, he passed a familiar-looking face. The man strode hastily away, not looking back. Porter suddenly realized who it was ... Francis Higbee. He turned his horse and rode back to catch up with him.

When Higbee saw who was following, he panicked and ran to a side street. Porter followed and rode up next to him, pulling out his loaded pepper revolver. He decided to get a little revenge — but without harming him. He pulled the trigger and fired — just over Higbee's head. Brick chips fell from a wall beside him and landed in his hair.

Higbee came to a stop.

"What do you want with me!" yelled Higbee.

"To send you to Hades, Higbee, nothing much."

CHAPTER 70

"All right, you've won," said Higbee. "So do it."

"I ain't won. You have the victory, Higbee. Joseph is dead, and our people have been driven out, just like you promised. I guess that makes you . . . the winner. So . . . 'You happy?"

"Go ahead — shoot me."

Porter merely chuckled.

Higbee stared at him, surprised and curious as Porter shook his head.

"For the rest of your life, Higbee, you will never know when you go to bed at night if an avenging angel is coming in your room to send you to your Maker."

Higbee's huge sallow face went even whiter. "Just get it over with."

"That's too easy. You need to wonder when it'll happen — if ever. And you need to know every single night the rest of your life that you have to be prepared to meet your Maker — and Joseph and all the other good folks you've inspired the mobs to kill — and then ask yourself if you're *really* ready."

"Just kill me now if you're going to!"

"Not on your life." Porter smiled at his irony. "And I want this same message delivered to the Laws, the Fosters, Joe Jackson, Charles Ivins, Henry Norton, John Hicks, Augustin Spencer and your brother. They'll have to go to bed the rest of their lives, too — maybe days, maybe months, maybe years — wondering when the avenging angel may strike. So Francis, you know I'm going to let you live at least a couple days till you get word around, now don't you?"

Higbee gulped, unsure what to say. "Maybe."

"Sure you do. You have my personal guarantee. In fact I want you to enjoy the next 48 hours. I promise during that time you will not have to worry about turning around and seeing who's following you, or walking a different way home from work. Why am I being so generous? I want you free from all these worries, so when you report to your friends you won't leave out any details. All right, Higbee?"

"Why are you doing this to me?" said Higbee.

"I like to see bad boys sweat." Porter then shot a hole in Higbee's hat and said, "Get out of here."

Higbee ran off, relieved for the moment, but as Porter rode away on his horse, he knew he had put the man in hell.

Porter missed the last ferry out of Nauvoo, sidetracked by the Higbee incident, so that night he slept in a hotel room. He placed a derringer under his pillow and kept his arsenal of weapons beside his bed, loaded.

In the middle of the night, his door burst open. By the time he pulled up his derringer, he was looking into the shotgun barrel of Sheriff Jacob Backenstos.

"You're under arrest, Porter."

"What the devil for?"

"Terrorizing Francis Higbee."

"How terrible," muttered Porter.

"Also for the murder of Frank Worrell."

"Worrell?" said Porter. "The same Worrell I saved your life from?"

Backenstos broke into a cold sweat.

"What if I put up a fight?" said Porter. "Would you shoot the man that saved you?"

"I wouldn't, but I've got six sharpshooters outside, and they're the best the state militia could offer — so I suggest you come peaceful."

Although Porter did not particularly want to, he knew he could take care of Backenstos, but the six sharpshooters outside were a different matter. Yet it was still worth a try, he thought. Then three deputies suddenly appeared behind the sheriff with pistols drawn. Porter lowered his derringer as he mumbled, "Gratitude."

CHAPTER 71

Porter awakened in jail, focusing first on Backenstos bringing him breakfast.

"I know what you're thinking, Porter."

"What am I thinking?"

"It's obvious from the look on your face," said the sheriff. "But I'm no traitor to you. 'Fact is, I agree with you. 'Other fact is, I'm testifying on your behalf on the Worrell murder charge. I was there, so you don't have to worry. As for Higbee's charge of terrorizing him, is that true?"

"Now would I terrorize a dung-eating lizard that eats his own kind?"

Backenstos smiled, "That's what I figured, so I'll recommend to the judge that Higbee had been drinking too much when he reported it."

Porter smiled back. He liked Backenstos after all. Sort of. Jail still wasn't his idea of a holiday.

After breakfast Almon Babbitt came to visit.

"How am I going to get you out of here?" said the wily, smart-mouthed attorney. Despite the man's narcissistic nature, Babbitt did hold a redeeming asset or two; Porter admired his competence and apparent loyalty to Brigham, even with his un-rivaled conceit. Yet in Porter's mind Babbitt's loyalty was still suspect especially since he had represented Joseph's enemies at Carthage. That one point was still a sharp burr in Porter's heel. And it didn't help that Babbitt had represented Luana for her divorce — especially on those outrageous charges, as Por-ter viewed them.

"I know what you're thinking," said Babbitt. "But Joseph never asked me for help at first, so I took the first available client to come along. It happened to be Joseph's enemies, but they didn't have a case in Hades — we both know that. Joseph would've gotten off scott free had his case gone to trial. So I took their stupidity all the way to the bank, so to speak." Bab-bitt smiled but Porter was too angry to talk.

"Now," said Babbitt, "you're wondering why I didn't drop those clients when Joseph's uncle finally did send for me to represent him. Correct?"

Porter merely stared at him, watching him verbally dig his own grave.

"Simple," answered Babbitt. "I know my clients would lose. There was no question. And I wasn't used to working under another attorney, as I would have with Woods — Joseph's chief attorney. So all in all, it worked out, don't you think?"

Porter still just gazed at him.

"All right," said Babbitt. "There's no love lost between us here. But let's change the subject to you for a moment. On this matter of Francis Higbee, could I ask a personal question? If you had to do it over again, you'd probably do it anyway, am I right?"

Porter did not change his expression.

"I can get the court held outside Hancock County if you'll agree to face a first degree murder charge."

Porter's eyes smoldered.

Babbitt read them and continued, "They've piled on other charges to keep you here — even counterfeiting — but I think I can get your case transferred to Galena, 150 miles north."

"Sorry." He doubted anything Babbitt claimed to be truthful and even wondered if Babbitt were setting a trap for him. But Babbitt's expression of concern rather surprised him. Maybe Babbitt *was* coming up with the best strategy for him. Brigham was certainly out for Porter's best interests and he had in fact sent Babbitt to help free him. Porter gazed at him with a long assessing look.

"Do you want a fair trial or not?"

Porter's expression finally melted.

"There's just one thing," added Babbitt. "At Galena they'll probably hold you in jail for a few months till the trial."

Porter flinched at the words.

CHAPTER 72

Four months later, Porter was still in jail. His case had been transferred to Galena, Illinois, all right, and now he was rotting in a cell on bread and water. Almon Babbitt was meanwhile busy with other clients in Nauvoo and had no reason to make a several day journey to him until right up to the day of the trial. Nor did he greatly suspect Porter's mistreatment. If he had, and if the truth be known, he probably would not have much cared. He was busy trying to make as much money as possible from wrapping up the legal and business affairs of the exodus and the sale of certain properties. Porter had requested through numerous letters for Babbitt to come visit him but Babbitt never did, and then it became apparent his messages were not leaving the jail. No one apparently knew his conditions nor had reasons for concern.

Babbutt could have guessed at the facts, but chose to ignore his own instincts, telling himself he was too busy to deal with Porter.

So once again, he was withering and, as in Missouri, he wondered if he were going to die. He had visions of Emily waiting for his return, probably worried sick over whether or not he was still even alive. He wondered if she had lived on the rugged plains journey to the Rocky Mountains. He had wanted to take her there himself, as well as the other children. He also wondered if Alpheas were kind to the children, and especially to Emily, the most sensitive of all. The idea of any mistreatment of her by Cutler cut Porter to the heart. He had to live to see her again.

The jailer entered one morning with a pot of hot turnip soup, minus the turnip, and chuckled as he informed Porter that his case had been forgotten by the court system; he would spend the rest of his life there.

Three days later he heard leather shoes clopping up the stairs. He heard a key enter the lock. The door opened and there stood a torch-lit figure. Jacob Backenstos, entering his cell.

"It's our day in court, Porter. My heavens, son, what have they done to you?"

Porter looked emaciated, and could barely walk. Backenstos unchained him, then helped him bathe, and finally assisted him into a change of clothes. Together they walked to the courthouse, Backenstos acting strangely silent.

Inside the packed courtroom were 200 curious townspeople there to see history — the death sentence of the most notorious desperado in U.S. history to date, according to the press. Porter, in chains, was led by Backenstos to his seat on the front pew. Across the room he beheld Francis Higbee seated with his brother, Chauncey, and 10 other conspirators. Porter slowly sat down, glowering at them. Backenstos sat to his right, then Babbitt entered and sat to his left, who immediately leaned to Porter and whispered, "Greetings, old friend. Stand when they announce the judge is entering."

Porter glared at him, wondering where the devil his help was the past four months in jail.

The judge entered, and the prosecuting attorney presented his case against Porter.

It was Backenstos' turn to sit on the stand and face the courtroom. Porter stared at him, knowing this one man had the complete ability to determine his future — and it was an uneasy feeling. What if the sheriff had been paid off to betray him? He wished he had abided Joseph's advice to never be placed in a position again to ever be taken prisoner by anyone.

CHAPTER 73

After being sworn in, Sheriff Backenstos told the jury and packed courtroom that if ever a man were innocent of charges, it was Porter Rockwell, as he personally was at the killing scene of Frank Worrell and saw Rockwell shoot Worrell only in self-defense.

Porter breathed out a sigh of relief and slunk down ever so slightly on the pew.

Backenstos further testified that he had actually *deputized* and ordered Porter to help him. Backenstos gazed across the silent, stunned courtroom and he knew he had swayed the crowd. Most in attendance were actually shocked. They had surmised a completely different story from the press reports. They had in fact been certain that the notorious Mormon outlaw would be nailed on first degree murder, and that Backenstos would back up *their* testimony.

Almon Babbitt studied the jury panel and smiled. He knew he had this one in the bag, and elbowed Porter under the table.

Porter then noticed Babbitt's sly smile tugging at the edge of his lips. Almon Babbitt was bright enough to then bring in a parade of witnesses who admitted seeing Worrell engaged in violent, anti-Mormon behavior. Babbitt finally wrapped up his summary with caustic questions about Worrell's character; his logic was flawless and his sardonic humor brilliant. Porter could see that Babbitt held them in the palm of his hands. Such a day in court to a man like Babbitt was downright delicious. In attorney lingo for the day, he *mauled* his opponent — the prosecutor and his team, including friends of Frank Worrell visiting from Carthage.

The chief prosecuting attorney finished his summary and the jury dismissed and quickly returned. The jury foreman handed a paper to the judge, who announced:

"Not guilty."

The courtroom erupted. Fully half the people — chiefly those visiting from Carthage and Warsaw — wanted Porter hung; the other half — and certainly all the jury — had been swayed entirely by Babbitt's oratory and the solid case he and Backenstos had presented.

The judge called for order. He then told Francis Higbee to voice his complaint for the other case against Porter.

Higbee accurately reported what had happened in the side street four months earlier, but embellished it with fantasies, describing in detail how Porter threatened to cut his throat and leave him to gasp for air and die, then walk away eating cake from Higbee's own kitchen. Porter smiled, pleased that Higbee's imagination had added that part. He was actually amazed that Higbee's propensity for distorting the truth could work so well to his benefit: Higbee would live out his days suffering more in his mind from his fears and his own embellishments than even what Porter had imagined.

The judge turned to Porter and said, "What say ye?"

"One question first, your honor," said Porter.

"Granted," said the judge.

Porter gazed across the courtroom and finally said, "Has Mr. Higbee been drinking?"

The courtroom erupted in laughter.

Backenstos then received permission from the court to speak. "Actually, at the time of his report, I did smell liquor on the plaintiff's breath, your honor. In fact if you'll look at the exhibit, his own affidavit when he reported the complaint shows he was on his way out of 'The Wayland Inn' tavern when he was confronted by Mr. Rockwell. I have nothing more to say."

Backenstos glanced at Porter with a smile behind his eyes. Porter glanced at Higbee with the same smile.

Higbee fumed.

The judge nodded to the jury, and they retired.

An hour later they returned with a verdict.

"Not guilty."

Higbee stood and shouted, "Why!"

The judge pounded his gavel, told Higbee to sit down, and answered him:

"Your case is dismissed on account of no witnesses, sir." The judge then glanced at Porter and caught him smiling at Higbee — he detected a mocking smile, and blurted out:

"Mr. Rockwell, I warn you to not terrorize good citizens anymore. I will not put up with your intimidating Mr. Higbee or anyone else formerly connected with Mr. Smith." The judge glanced at the jury, and back at Porter, "Whether you have done so yet or not. " He regarded Porter a moment longer and continued, "I sense a contempt within you for either this court or the plaintiff Mr. Higbee, or both, and I hereby order you out of the county, and recommend you join your people moving Westward before there is further trouble."

Porter faked a smile at the judge, who was disconcerted by it. The judge was correct: Porter held absolute contempt for not only Higbee and company but for a judicial system which failed to provide any protection whatsoever for his people, for Joseph, and — during his last four months in jail — for himself. He took one last long look at the judge and smirked, then glanced at Higbee and, with his back to the magistrate so the magistrate could not see him, he pointed his finger at Higbee as if aiming a pistol, and winked.

Higbee's eyes went wide.

A hundred people shouted at Porter for his overt threat, but the judge, not seeing it, pounded his gavel, threatening to fine everyone making noise in the courtroom.

Porter turned to the crowd with a little wave and a smile. A couple dozen who sided with him chuckled.

While he strutted past Higbee, he muttered to Higbee's group, as he smiled, "Remember the angel."

CHAPTER 74

Higbee quaked at Porter's words. As did his brother, Chauncey. As did the Fosters, the Laws, Augustin Spencer, Charles Ivins, Henry Norton, John Hicks, and Joe Jackson, all sitting in the courtroom to lend their support to Francis Higbee, but wishing they had never attended.

Porter was still smiling when he came out of the courtroom into the fresh clear day. Sheriff Backenstos accompanied him, along with Davies County Sheriff Tom Mackelby, who stopped and handed Porter his confiscated weapons but no ammunition.

"Why no ammunition?" said Porter.

"It's for your own good."

"What about my horse?"

"Keeping it for court expenses."

"Court expenses?"

"Ain't my idea," said Mackelby.

Porter snorted with anger, then Almon Babbitt appeared around the corner with another horse.

"I was prepared for such contingencies," said Babbitt. "But it'll cost you your gold watch."

Porter scowled at him, remembering Luana's picture was inside the top lid of the watch. He realized he had no need for it anymore, despite its help in getting him through nine months of jail in Missouri three years earlier. It nevertheless pulled a heartstring as he handed the watch over to Babbitt. Porter gazed with a certain emptiness at the watch, and then at the animal.

"Nice horse," said Backenstos. "You attached to yours like I am to mine?"

"I confess I am," said Porter. It had been given him by Joseph on Christmas Eve after his jail experience.

Backenstos turned to Sheriff Mackelby, "I see no reason why a little trade can't be made here; do you, Sheriff?"

The Davies County sheriff nodded and switched horses — Porter got his old horse back and Mackelby got the new horse that Almon Babbitt had brought.

As Porter mounted his horse he received several days travel rations from the two sheriffs' saddlebags, then glanced back gratefully and nodded. He noticed a glimmer of admiration in their eyes, and rode off in a good round trot, once again feeling new life.

Backenstos, Mackelby and Babbitt watched him disappear around the bend of a deserted, country road. Babbitt then admired his new gold watch. Snapping it open, he beheld the picture of Luana inside the top. He looked up curiously. "Porter, you forgot something."

Porter was surprised when Babbitt actually caught up to him and handed back his watch. Porter smiled slightly — in both gratitude and satisfaction at seeing Babbitt turn away from a gold watch — all for a mere sentimental reason.

Porter nodded and took the watch, winked at Babbitt, then turned away.

Deeper around the woodland bend, he realized he was out of even Babbitt's sight, so he stopped at a narrow river. He took out the watch and gazed at Luana's old picture one last time. Then, feeling both exhileration from the freedom he felt by his *choice* to cut the last emotional tie, and the pain he simultaneously felt from his sudden, resurfacing feelings, he threw the watch as far out into the river as he could, then resumed walking.

Rain had fallen and the scent of the air tasted fine. As Porter passed a farm, he noted the smell of the freshly turned earth. He felt a determination to never again take the taste of free air for granted. As fun as it felt, it just wasn't worth it to exact revenge for the sake of revenge. Ever again.

CHAPTER 75

As Porter rode across Nauvoo on Mulholland he scanned the strangely quiet streets that had once teemed with commerce and thousands of families . . . and for an instant he pictured Joseph Smith atop his steed beside the Mansion House . . .

Porter thought he saw a twelve-year-old boy beside the house. He wondered if he were imagining Joseph as a lad . . . he even heard the boy's voice calling. He suddenly recognized Joseph Smith III running towards him and climbing a fence.

Porter dismounted and the boy hugged him.

"You're not coming West, Joseph?"

"Our family's staying."

Porter was saddened Emma had not left with Brigham's people to Iowa. He gazed again at the nearly-deserted streets and felt a bizarre sensation. With a pain in his chest he studied Joseph's son. The resemblance was strong enough to remind him of his childhood days when he and Joseph would play together on their farms in New York.

"Oh Joseph, Joseph," said Porter, "they've killed the only friend I've ever had."

Young Joseph saw tears on Porter's face.

"I suppose it will do you no good," Porter continued, "if anyone sees you with me. It could only get you in trouble. Enemies of our people still hunt me. Be off with you, boy."

Young Joseph walked slowly away, turning back several times to study his father's friend. (Author's note: Details and dialogue of this scene are verbatim as later reported by Joseph Smith III.)

Porter led his horse toward the Nauvoo House Dock Landing at the south end of Nauvoo. As he approached the Nauvoo Hotel, he stopped and gazed across the city. On the hazy September landscape he pondered, at once calm and disturbed over who might have seen the boy with him. He actually feared for Joseph's boy.

He walked toward the dock and eyed the ferry that would take him to Iowa. It was making its way across the river towards him for its final afternoon run. Before he went down the hill, he turned again to face the city, and this time could not remove his eyes from the scene: They rested on the Mansion House, with Joseph on the porch, gently smiling at friends. Joseph looked up and smiled at Porter. Then Porter noticed Joseph suddenly in different clothes, standing proudly in his legionnaire uniform hailing his hundreds of troops, with Porter himself on the front line.

Young Joseph III, a block away, stared at the man at the edge of town and, in his final glimpse of Orrin Porter Rockwell, saw Porter mysteriously salute someone apparently standing in front of the Mansion House, and then turn away for his final walk on Nauvoo soil, striding directly toward the barge.

It would be Porter's last view of the wide, mid-western rivers he so loved, on a type of boat — a ferryboat — that once so captured his imagination. And it would take him across the Mississippi River for the final time in his life.

CHAPTER 76

By September 1846 when Porter was released from Galena, Illinois, nearly all the Mormons who had planned to leave Nauvoo were evacuated. But the last 700 experienced the most traumatic exodus of all.

The bulk of the Saints were making their way to Winter Quarters, Nebraska, their new temporary headquarters. They had moved their base of operations from Council Bluffs, Iowa months earlier.

But these final 700 immigrants from Nauvoo were too poor or too ill to move across the river. Some of these unfortunates were recent converts who had spent all their means just to get to Nauvoo and were now, for all practical purposes, broke.

By late August 1846, mobbers had increased their pressure on these final 700 and actually attacked them. The four-day series of battles killed several Saints and was dubbed the "Battle of Nauvoo." The remaining immigrants surrendered and were made to cross the river to Montrose, Iowa.

There, all 700 were camped along the Mississippi River. Many lacked even a tent to protect them from rainstorms, much less a wagon to carry them Westward. With little food among them, many starved and died from exposure within days.

News of this reached Brigham and he immediately sent wagons of supplies storming across the prairie. A volunteer rescue crew with 20 wagons, 41 cows, and 17 oxen arrived at the distressed saints, and found them barely alive. They fed them, rounded them up, placed them in wagons of mercy, and brought them across the prairie. On October 6, 1846 they arrived at Winter Quarters.

Three days later, the entire main camp of Winter Quarters was also experiencing a dire need for food. As the children of Israel had miraculously been fed manna in the wilderness in Biblical times, a flock of quail landed in the Mormons' camp. The wild game were exhausted and easy to catch, saving the day for many.

When he had more supplies and volunteers gathered, Brigham then sent a second rescue mission, which arrived at the Mississippi River in late October.

By November 1846 all those too enfeebled and poor to flee but who wanted to go west were now safely at Winter Quarters, where they waited for spring to begin the cross-country trek.

Meanwhile, upon his release from Galena Jail, Porter rode toward the sun. Two weeks later he arrived at the western border of the Iowa territory at Council Bluffs. There, he found Brigham Young and other Mormon leaders in William Clayton's tent. They beheld him as he entered, ceased all conversation, and shook his hand. A smile glistened in Brigham's eyes, seeing Porter safely returned from the most dangerous county on earth.

Porter knew he was back among friends. He was satisfied also to note that a place within Brigham's heart was growing for him. He then learned from Brigham that 500 of their healthiest young men had been recruited by the U. S. Army for service in the Mexican War, despite the fact they desperately needed these men to aid in the wagon migration West. True, they were being reimbursed financially, but it likely was not offset by the loss of healthy bodies for their greatest physical challenge to date — the trek West. Even though they had been driven out of the U.S., Brigham had fully cooperated in the recruitment.

"The Mormon Battalion will honor us, Porter. We will prove our loyalty to the country, despite our exile."

"We oughta march the 500 boys on the Carthage Greys is what we oughta do," said Porter, "If you wanna talk about honor."

The Battalion had left weeks earlier while Porter was in jail, and would end its journey in California, Brigham added. Then he surprised him:

"I'm very, very sorry to say this, Porter."

Porter stared, waiting for a painful announcement.

"Luana and Alpheas are remaining in Iowa. Certain Saints are figuring the trip too difficult, and even though they had the fortitude to leave their possessions in Nauvoo, they can't bring themselves to take the final step with us to the mountains."

Porter stared at him, terrified about not seeing his children and thoroughly distressed over their future away from the kingdom.

Brigham noted only one movement in Porter's face — the muscles under his eyes winced.

CHAPTER 77

Porter galloped toward Luana's campsite. He arrived at their hut and Emily ran out to embrace him. Porter kissed her and strode to the door. The other children came out and greeted him reluctantly with hugs. He noticed Luana was slow to respond to his arrival by not yet greeting him, so he decided to play with the children awhile, although he sensed their earlier coolness growing even stronger.

A half hour passed, when Porter decided to see Luana. He knocked on the door. Luana slowly answered, merely opening it a crack and glancing at him.

"You packed up and ready?" said Porter with forced enthusiasm.

"You must've heard," said Luana.

"I must have."

She opened the door and invited him in.

"I'm taking at least the children with me," said Porter. "How you and Alpheas throw your lives down the ditch is up to you."

"Why are you so determined to make life hard on everybody?"

"Brigham ordered us to go West," said Porter, "and I follow him. It's that simple."

"It's not that simple."

"Alpheas isn't in the best of health for traveling."

"Neither is a few thousand other souls who are going."

"Nobody knows how hard it is to travel those plains and passes — only mountain men and Indians have done it before now."

"That is a good reason. If you're looking for one not to go. But we go. I don't argue with Brigham."

"That pretty much defines the difference between us, doesn't it, Porter?"

He gazed at her a long moment and finally realized how accurate her assessment was. She nodded and smiled reassuringly, seeing him finally understand what she herself had come to accept about herself.

Cutler came into the hut, overhearing from outside. "Porter, you are perhaps forgetting one thing here. We have a choice to follow Brigham or not."

"Like the children of Israel could choose to follow Moses or not," replied Porter, imploring Cutler since he knew Luana was not going to bend. "You can choose to not follow like they, and wonder around in Iowa's wilderness for forty years, or make the right choice. I choose to follow, and I'm taking the kids with me if you choose to stay."

"Porter," broke in Luana, "the children want to stay as well."

Cutler smiled, "There is no way on God's green earth any of us are going. So give it up."

Porter was aghast. He turned to Luana. "They've been listening to you and Alpheas so they don't see the picture clear."

"For what they do see, they see clearly enough," said Luana.

"It's true, Daddy," spoke Porter's second oldest daughter, now entering with the other children. "Can you stay with us here?"

"That can't happen, honey." Porter turned to Luana. "'It makes me sick hearin' this kinda talk."

"They're old enough to think for themselves. They've heard stories of how harsh the Great Basin is. No trees, no water . . . Indians . . . "

"We plant trees and we irrigate," retorted Porter. "And I take care of the Indians."

"Porter, they've made their decision," reiterated Cutler.

Porter decided to talk to Emily last. He turned to his other children. "Are any of you kids going with me, or do you want to stay here with your Mama?"

They each walked to their mother to answer his question.

"Porter," said Luana, "they really do see Alpheas as their father now. You were gone so much in their early years, they don't know you as well."

"And Emily?" said Porter.

"Emily also."

"Maybe Emily can tell us that for herself," said Porter.

Emily smiled at him, "Mama always gets her way with us, doesn't she?"

Luana felt the subtle barb, and reacted. "But Mama looks after us best, in the end, doesn't she?"

Emily looked down. "In some ways I can't disagree with that."

Porter suddenly wondered if Luana had pressured, threatened, or somehow altered her thinking. For years he had no doubt he was the favored of the two, but now had sudden doubts as to what had transpired the previous few months. Had Luana talked her into seeing him as unworthy as a father, because of spending time in jail with his name splashed all over area newspapers as a notorious outlaw? He felt sickened. He turned to Emily. "Well?"

They all turned to her. Her moment of decision had come.

CHAPTER 78

Emily slowly gazed back and forth between Luana and Porter.

Porter wondered if — even if she did still prefer to be with him — could she stand up to her mother's strong presence and disagree with her.

Emily knew if she chose Porter, there would be Hades to pay even in the few weeks before she would leave, as she needed her mom to help her make clothes for travelling. Her mother would in her subtle manner throw tantrums, some silent, others overt, and she'd layer that with showering Emily with guilt for leaving her. Emily had no doubt she had her pa's encouragement, but the control she felt from her mother was too much against which to stand.

"Well?" said Luana to Emily.

"I'm going with Papa," said Emily.

Porter beamed. He felt like cheering.

"We need to talk, honey," said Luana to her.

Alpheas tried concealing a smile, and retired into the other room, knowing the outcome of this battle.

"Before I talk with Emily, I want to speak with you," said Luana to Porter, taking his arm and escorting him out back.

There, she spoke softly. "We all know how Emily adores you, and I'm certain you're flattered, but you should know I've given this much thought, and I feel very strongly she should stay with us — at least until she's older."

It was all pretty predictable to Porter, but he met her head on. "Are you crazy? Why should I leave her if she wants to go and I also want her to?"

Luana shook her head, challenging his sanity more subtly. "What will you do when you arrive there?"

"What do you mean what will I do?"

"I know you haven't given it much thought," she said, "but I have. You'll forever be doing things Brigham wants you to — adventure — travel — probably gunplay."

"No more gunplay. I have thought that much out."

"In any case you'll be going on dangerous assignments, correct? You said something about Indians? Even if these are peace missions to the Indians, can't we agree there's some danger we're talking about? What kind of life is that for a child? And what if you decide to not take her on an assignment and you don't come back to her — what if something happens to you out there? Where will she turn to then?"

"My ma and sisters would take care of her."

"They're not the same as her parents," said Luana.

"I said I'd look after her."

"And I'm saying what if you're at the end of your nine lives?

She belongs with me, Porter. You leave her where she belongs. She'll be happy here with brothers, sisters and her mama, and we'll keep her protected and well fed. I'm not certain you can do that, and I doubt you are either."

Porter suspected she was right, and looked down again. Luana left him alone to think as long as he needed and she returned to the hut. He considered her words as he ambled out to a slow-moving stream behind their campsite and thought about it for fully three hours. He tossed a rock in the water and watched its rings ripple out from the center. He was torn as he'd never been in his life. He finally traipsed back to the hut.

Emily greeted him and hugged his waist. "When can we go, Papa?"

"We can't."

"What do you mean?"

Luana arrived and looked at them both, tears streaming down her face for Emily's disappointment.

"Your mama's right, honey," said Porter. "You gotta stay."

"No, Papa!"

"I'm going to be doing dangerous things. You need your schooling and family to be with you. I wouldn't be around for you."

"I don't care — I'll go with you, just like we've always done."

"You're getting closer to the age where you need more learning about society and the world that your mama can give you, and preparing yourself to be a grown, young lady."

"I'm almost grown already," she said. "Thirteen's old enough to decide where I can go!"

"I wish that was true," said Porter. "You're sure a big young lady, but you're at a real important age the next few years, and that's when you'll decide where you'll go with your life and what you grow up to be. You need your mama and family to help you so you decide things with the right people around you."

Emily began crying. "I need to be with you."

Porter choked back tears, walking away, "You need to be with family."

"You are my family."

Porter walked faster to get away, and she ran to him and he picked her up, kissing her tear-drenched cheek.

Porter, still holding and squeezing her, gazed through glistening eyes at Luana and Alpheas and the other three children, then became composed enough to speak:

"I expect letters from the kids every month the rest of their lives or I'm coming back to get them. 'That clear?"

Alpheas answered, "That's very clear, and I think we can agree to that."

Porter blurted out, "I don't give a rat's rear if you agree, she's got to agree." Porter shot his look at Luana, who nodded in agreement.

Porter set down Emily and picked up each child and kissed them, then strode to his horse. He mounted up and quickly rode away.

Emily was surprised he would not look back at her, and ran after him.

Porter glanced back and saw her running behind. He picked up his gait, tears flowing down both his cheeks.

She yelled, "Papa!"

But he kept riding. He heard her calling out through tears,